Bane of the Innocent

Gray Door Ltd.

ISBN 978-1-945530-90-6

Contents

Chapter one: Cherub Adrift 1

Chapter Two: Two of a kind.................................... 14

Chapter Three: Here's a Plan 23

Chapter Four: The Storm 32

Chapter Five: The Remnants................................ 45

Special Bonus Story

Twelve Minutes till Midnight 53

Chapter one: Cherub Adrift

The sounds of cannon and rifles firing in the distance accompanied Sammy as he opened his eyes from a night of sleep. He'd become accustomed to these sounds, as well as the marching soldiers, galloping horses and other implements of war moving back and forth on the roads around him. These sounds had become somewhat comforting to the young boy and made him feel less lonesome.

What bothered his young mind more than anything was waking to see the beady eyes that now stared at him with a violent intent. The creature hissed and threatened a fight over the apple core he'd been saving for when those pains in his stomach returned. This creature had lately become a constant nuisance to Sammy and forced him to bring a large stick to bed with him. ¶Along with the threat of stealing his last morsel of food, the large raccoon facing the scruffy seven year old boy also threatened to give away his sleeping spot under the large house.

Sammy slowly moved his hand down until he took hold of the stick lying beside his leg; he then lifted it to the face of the hissing raccoon. He didn't want to strike the creature and cause a ruckus that might be heard in the house above.

The masked bandit hissed violently at the stick, seeming reluctant to give up the prospect of an apple core. He then nudged the raccoon with the makeshift weapon, causing it to snap at it, hissing and biting it. Sammy's heart beat faster, but he didn't back down. He'd faced this particular raccoon before and ended up losing a scrap of food to him. In this confrontation however, Sammy held the stick as well as the apple core.

The raccoon again tried to advance. Again Sammy blocked the attack with the stick. Frustrated by this new weapon the young boy had at his disposal, the raccoon reluctantly conceded and scampered on, searching other nooks and crannies for insects and grubs.

Once the raccoon ventured far enough away, Sammy put the stick down. From the jumbled up rags that made his bed he pulled the brown fragments of an apple core. Rolling onto his back he began chewing on the core and examining the bottom of the floor directly above him.

As he finished the apple remnants, the young boy listened to the sounds of war in the distance and the sounds of footsteps walking across the floor. He listened closely to the sounds indicating people were close by.

His bed of rags lay beside the base of the fireplace. He also found it comforting to be by the rocks. Sammy rolled over against the bedrocks, putting an arm on one of them as if snuggling up to a parent.

After a few moments, the effects of his tiny meal began to wear off and he knew he must get out.

He crawled along a worn path to the edge of the house. Peering from under the structure to make sure he wouldn't be seen, the young lad scrambled out and made his way along the back of the large two story building and to its corner. From there he again scanned around to be sure no one was close by. Then, he quickly made a dash for the outhouse.

First he ran to the back, to ensure no one occupied the small building. He knew he would need to do his business quickly, so once inside he did what he had to and then darted back out and to the corner of the house again.

He'd been through this same routine many times before and the young boy moved cautiously but deliberately around to the back door. He peeked under the bottom to spot anyone inside.

Once this had been done, he quietly opened the door and crept in. Once inside, he moved to the kitchen and hid under a cupboard, behind a large piece of cloth used to cover it. From there he could peer out on the morning's activity.

Soon, Sara came into the kitchen carrying a basket with some small apples. She went through them, wiping each one off and checking for worms; as she did many mornings lately.

Apples had become one of the food items still somewhat available in Atlanta. She picked the worst of the bunch and sat it on the counter. Sammy knew she'd sat the small bruised apple there for him. He also knew she could get into trouble for doing so.

With the war all around now, obtaining enough food had become a problem for everyone. Sammy heard Madam Francine say the task of feeding all the "girls" had become much more difficult to do.

Until a few months past, he'd been able to stay in a back room of the house. But now his mother had become worse than before. Madam Francine often called his mother a "drunk." His mother also used the medicine in the small bottles more often, along with drinking from the large bottles.

Lately his mother seldom came out of her room. She would use the outhouse and then go back to her bed. Madam Francine would make her bathe, but would always shout at his mother while she did so.

Sammy had become more concerned about his mother's care for him as he'd once heard some of the other "girls" as Madam Francine called them, talking about him. They didn't know he was close by as they spoke.

They said Madam Francine had told Sammy's mother to give him away after he was born. His mother had trouble finding a home for him and after a while insisted on keeping him. This was when Madam Francine began to dislike his mother.

Eventually, Madam Francine made Sammy get out of the house altogether as food became scarcer. She told him his mother wasn't working to pay her own way, much less his. Sammy now found himself hiding from her and fending for himself.

His mother seemed unaware of the problems her son was having. Often when Sammy talked to her, she didn't appear to understand anything he said.

He now found himself longing for the time when he could stay in the house and eat leftovers from the table. He would always try very hard to remain unseen by the "clients" as Madam Francine generally called them. This now seemed to be a dream to him as day by day things became more difficult for everyone and there were no longer any leftovers from the table.

Many men visited the large house and it was clear to Sammy he'd become more of a problem for Madam Francine in respect to those visitors.

Sara however still had a soft spot for the young boy and tried to leave bits of food for him, out of the kindness of her heart.

She left the kitchen with the other apples and Sammy quickly darted out of the cupboard to retrieve the small prize. He then moved into the large reception room and ever so quietly dashed under the stairwell. He hid in a small nook that had become one of his favorite spots.

Safely tucked under the stairwell, he took a small bite of the apple. He then waited patiently. After a few minutes Sara came to the edge of the stairwell just as Madam Francine began to ascend it and they met in the middle.

"Are the girls ready Sara?"

"Yes, fairly so Madam. Except for MS Elsa, I don't think she even understands the situation."

Madam Francine let out a disgruntled sigh upon hearing this. Sammy listened closer as he knew they were speaking of his mother.

"She's becoming more trouble than she's worth. If not for the soldiers who only want to pay with that worthless paper money, I would toss her out. And that little rodent of hers is still around somewhere I'm sure; likely stealing food.

"Well, never mind her Sara. Commissioner Franks said the Yankees could break through any day now.

"I realize riding in the back of his wagon will be unusual for the girls but it's the best we can do and he's very gracious to offer. To have access to horses of any kind is rare these days. Have all the girls ready first thing in the morning.

"If that worthless cow in the corner room isn't ready then she'll just get to meet the Yankees when they arrive."

"Yes Madam," Sara replied.

Sammy pretended he didn't hear Madam Francine call his mother a worthless cow. In fact, he had drifted away from the conversation right after becoming aware that his mother was being bad mouthed. This seemed to make him feel better.

Rather than listen to Madam Francine talk bad about his mother, Sammy observed a small worm crawl out of the apple he held. Instead of letting the worm crawl out of the apple, he would touch it on its head and force the worm to go back into the apple.

He amused himself this way until Sara and Madam Francine stopped talking. He then took another small bite, eating the worm as well as the apple. He'd recently become less worried about what he ate as hunger impacted his daily life.

When Sara and Madam Francine had left the stairway, Sammy crept out and moved with purpose up the stairs. He cautiously walked along the rail till reaching a room in the corner. He then ran his fingers through his dusty blonde hair several times and tapped on the door.

After a few seconds Sammy slowly opened the door. He'd been surprised and quite startled before by a man in the room with his mother.

When he could see her lying on the bed alone he called out softly.

"Ma... Ma," He walked into the room and quietly shut the door behind him. With his apple in hand he stood gazing at his motionless mother on the bed.

She almost appeared to be dead as she lay sprawled out with her hair a mess. Sammy often worried that he would come in one day to see her lying on the bed such as this and not be able to wake her. He shook his head in an effort to shoo away such thoughts.

The boy reached down and touched her arm. She felt warm so he knew she must be alive.

Again he brushed his dirty and unkempt hair with his fingers. He tried to knock some of the dust off of his clothes that were too small for him.

"Ma, it's me Sammy," he said in a hushed voice. His mother turned her head towards him.

"Sammy, can you run the chickens out of here?"

He examined the small room and saw no chickens.

"What do you mean, Ma?"

His mother mumbled something inaudible.

"I don't know what you said Ma."

"The chickens...I can't sleep with the chickens in here," she replied with frustration, in a louder voice.

Sammy now realized she must have drank too much of her medicine.

After some thought the boy replied, "Alright Ma, I'm getting the chickens out now."

His mother smiled and drifted back to sleep.

He sat down on the bed and continued taking small bites of his apple. He wanted to eat fast but if he ate slow and chewed a lot of times he seemed to be a little less hungry after he finished. He always seemed to think about food, but by taking smaller bites he made the food he had last longer.

As he sat on the edge of the bed, glancing down at his mother and thinking of these things, the sound of someone walking up the stairs and moving towards the room startled him. He quickly dodged under the bed as quietly as he could. Madam Francine soon came into the room.

"Else, you need to get up, do you hear me?" Madam Francine then began telling his mother about everyone going out of town for a while and something about the Yankees.

His mother sat up in the bed and seemed to be listening to her. All Sammy could see from under the bed was her feet and legs; he wasn't for certain how awake his mother actually was.

Then he heard her tell Madam Francine, "I'm not going anywhere without my Sammy." This made him feel good inside and for a few seconds he heard nothing else the two women said.

Soon however the hard floor and trying not to move brought him back to the real world.

He lay as still as any young boy could under the bed. He tried to think of anything to help him avoid moving and alerting Madam Francine. He tried to remember a time when he didn't have to hide under the bed.

There was a time he could still remember when his mother didn't sleep all the time. A time that now seemed long ago, when she didn't drink so much or take so much of her medicine. He laid there thinking about the happier time when he didn't get so hungry and so lonely under the big house.

Madam Francine's shoes moved back and forth as she now called his mother terrible names.

Sammy tried to use his memories of better times to block the harsh situation he now found himself in. He pulled the remnants of his apple close to his chest and though he tried to not let them out, a few tears welled up in his eyes and trickled down his cheek. He chided himself within for being weak and crying.

Finally, exhausted from the harsh language used against his mother, Madam Francine walked out, slamming the door behind her. His mother fell back into bed, unaware her son had been under it the entire time.

After a few moments, Sammy eased out from under the bed. Gazing down at his mother the boy wanted to hug her. But he knew she wouldn't even know he was there. He turned and crept out the door and quickly down the stairs, then on out the back.

A dusty heat swirled around as Sammy made his way through the streets of Atlanta. Soldiers moved to and fro, and horses with cannons rolled behind noisily. He liked the busy streets. The streets had not always been this busy, but the young boy had trouble remembering Atlanta before the war. As far back as he could recall he'd observed soldiers move about the streets.

More recently he observed what looked to be thousands of soldiers around Atlanta and could hear gunfire in the distance. Throughout the day cannon fire would also drop randomly into the city.

Sammy had once overheard some men talking of a girl about his age that was blown up by a mortar shell. He thought about the poor girl while he finished the apple that had now become brown and dusty. He wasted none of it, even eating the seeds.

As the young boy rounded the corner of a building, a familiar, though much despised voice came to his attention.

"Well, well, look here, it's an ugly little bastard."

Sammy immediately recognized the voice of Terence Osbrine.

Terence had cultivated a deep dislike and almost hate from Sammy as no other person in Atlanta, or around Atlanta for that matter, had been able to achieve. He beat up on Sammy as well as verbally abusing him almost every time they crossed paths.

Recently however, Sammy had proven he could run faster than Terence, so he generally just bad mouthed the young boy, otherwise the abuse would likely still be of a physical nature.

Sammy automatically stepped back in a defensive move, just in case he needed to run.

With the morning sun behind them, Terence and two other brutes stood staring ominously down at Sammy. He felt these two boys must surely be attracted to Terence and each other by their particular mean nature.

"This little bastard's mother works at Madam Francine's whore house."

When Terence said this, the other two boys laughed out loud.

Sammy stared at the three older boys without saying anything. Terence appeared to be older than the fifteen years Sammy had heard him to be. The other two may have been thirteen or fourteen years old but to him they all three looked old enough to be threatening.

"Where do you think you're going, you little bastard?" One of the other boys seemed anxious to prove he could dish out the punishment as well.

"I'm not going anywhere." Sammy replied meekly. All three laughed at his answer, as if he'd told a joke.

"No you're not going anywhere, because little bastards like you got no place to go do you?" Terence laughed again after he said this and the other two joined in.

Then he said, "Come on, we'll get that little runt later." With this comment the three walked off and Sammy felt relieved knowing Terence must have other things to do.

Realizing the bullies had been somewhat correct about him having no place to go, Sammy decided to sit down and consider where he might want to go.

The sporadic sound of gunfire and cannon in the distance seemed to keep time with the soldiers marching tiredly by. Then soldiers on horses moved by quickly as if in a hurry to get somewhere.

The people of Atlanta also moved about with a sense of purpose, but quietly and always making way for the soldiers. Their faces were gaunt and serious; carrying bags and having the appearance of despair.

Sammy finally grew weary of watching the people. All of them seemed mad or sad but none seemed to be happy. Not once did he see anyone smile. He sometimes wondered if he would ever see anyone smile again, other than Terence when he made fun of him.

Terence may smile about other people's pain but not Sammy. He wouldn't become a brute like that he thought to himself, as the dust from a passing wagon fluttered about him.

Then, he got the idea to go see his friend Tommy. He jumped up and made his way through the dust towards the edge of town.

Along the way he recalled meeting Tommy as the young soldier marched through. Sammy also sat by the street that day; when he heard someone call out to him. He lifted his head to find a small piece of salted pork flying towards him.

After retrieving the small treasure, Sammy followed Tommy as far as he could and watched from a distance until he could talk with him.

Eventually he found out where he'd been posted on guard duty. Since that day he'd ventured out on several occasions to the isolated guard post during the times he knew Tommy would be on guard duty.

The scruffy little boy stealthily avoided the sentries on the road by going through a wooded area to reach the outpost.

Every time he visited, Tommy would find some morsel of his food to share with the young boy. Sammy crept quietly through the brush and trees.

Finally he reached the edge of the wooded area and peered out over a small field. There, on the other side could be seen the dirt and timber earth works that had been built up by the army.

Sammy checked again to make sure he wouldn't be seen crossing the field and then moved across at trotting speed. Once he reached the earth works he called out to Tommy before going over and into the trench.

"It's me Tommy, don't shoot." Sammy had been told by the young soldier to do this so he wouldn't get shot; being mistaken for a Yankee.

Rolling over the mound, Sammy slid into the large trench. The smell of freshly dug dirt filled his nostrils.

"Sammy boy," Tommy appeared happy to see his little friend. The young man must have been sixteen or seventeen, Sammy didn't know for sure as he'd never asked. Every time he saw Tommy though, he appeared to have aged.

"Things are getting hot around here Sammy, you best be careful." The young soldier peeked over the top of the trench nervously.

"Most of the heavy stuff sounds to be off to the northeast over there, but I think the fighting might be moving this way. It's hard to know anymore as it moves around these days."

Sammy heard Tommy but he paid little attention to what he said. The boy's stomach reminded him now that the tiny breakfast he ate earlier had long lost its power.

Tommy leaned his musket against the log timbers lining part of the earth works.

"It's those sharpshooters you got to watch out for," he said as he sat down. The gunfire behind Tommy crackled and popped along with what sounded like occasional cannon fire.

"You hear that Sammy?" Tommy pointed his thumb backwards. "Sarge says a lot of that's sharpshooters trying to pick our boys off."

The young soldier then reached into his coat pocket and pulled out a small folded piece of cloth. Sammy eyed the item in Tommy's hands knowing there must be some food inside. "Ain't much here Sammy boy; a little hardtack is all I got. The rumor is our whole army's on half rations. Those Yankees got this area pinned down and not much is getting in."

Tommy broke a piece of the hardtack off and handed the small morsel to Sammy.

He took the piece of what appeared to be flat, hard bread. The hardtack had an appropriate name as the boy could barely get a bite from it. Yet as he chewed and swallowed small pieces, the pain in his stomach began to subside and he immediately felt better.

The sun appeared brighter and though still aware of the hot humid day, Sammy began to smile a little. When Tommy noticed Sammy smile he also smiled and began to relax as he chewed on a small piece of the hardtack.

"I'll be glad when this here war is over Sammy boy. I can't wait to eat some of my Ma's cooking again. My Ma has to be the best cook in Georgia. Well, least ways that's what I think anyhow. Is your Ma a good cook too, Sammy?"

The slight smile melted from Sammy's face when Tommy asked him this. The boy gazed down at the fragment of hardtack in his hand and tried to remember anything his mother had ever cooked.

"Well, I suppose so," Sammy replied. He thought all mothers must be good cooks, even though he couldn't think of anything his ma had ever cooked.

"Mm hmm, I'll bet she is Sammy. You should taste my Ma's cooking though, oh boy." The young soldier smiled and peered out into the air as if remembering the taste of his mother's cooking.

"My ma didn't want me to join up." Tommy's smile faded as he said this.

"But, we've not heard from my Pa for over a year now. We ain't got any more letters from him since Shiloh. I told Ma I should join up to help get this war over; then I can go find Pa. I figure he's in a prisoner camp somewhere."

Tommy somberly gazed down at the dirt. Sammy watched his friend with curiosity as he seemed to be talking to Sammy, but also appeared to be speaking with himself. He took another small bite of the hardtack as Tommy continued.

"I hated to leave that note for her, but I had to join up, you know what I'm saying don't ya, Sammy?"

The young boy had the feeling Tommy wanted him to condone leaving his mother a note and going off to war.

Sammy thought he must be right having a desire to help get the war over and go find his pa. He nodded in agreement with Tommy, and then took another tiny bite from the hardtack.

This made Tommy smile again and they both relaxed and ate the small morsels while sporadic gunfire crackled through the air in the distance.

After visiting Tommy for several hours, Sammy left him so he could do his soldiering.

Once more he trotted across the small field. He again dodged the other sentries by skirting through the woods. Sammy then casually made his way back into town. His stomach still complained, so as he walked through the streets he decided to go see Mr. Henry.

Mr. Henry owned a general store and on several occasions he sent Sammy on errands.

After the errand, he would give the boy some fruit or other small treat.

Sammy dodged through the people and soldiers moving about. Once, he almost got ran over by a wagon that appeared to be in a great hurry. The driver cursed Sammy very harshly and yelled at him to get out of the road.

Finally the boy came up to the general store. He could almost taste a piece of hard candy now. Surely there would be something the store keeper needed him to do.

Mr. Henry stood outside his store holding a board across the front window. He hammered a nail in as Sammy strolled up to him.

"Hello Mr. Henry."

"Oh, uh, hello Sammy," Mr. Henry replied as he glanced down from his work.

The boy watched as the storekeeper then put another board up to the window and began pounding a nail in. After he finished nailing one side of the board up Mr. Henry finally peered down at Sammy and gave him his full attention.

"Is there something I can do for you Sammy?"

"I wondered if you had an errand I could run for you Mr. Henry."

The storekeeper seemed puzzled by Sammy's question. He then turned and went back to nailing the other side of the board up.

"No, Sammy I'm sorry, I don't have anything for you right now. In fact you should probably go home, I suspect your folks will want you close by."

Sammy heard little after the "No, Sammy I'm sorry, I don't have anything for you." His head and spirit sank immediately upon hearing this.

"Alright," he strolled off through the busy streets, paying little attention to where he went.

Chapter Two: Two of a kind

Though Sammy had no awareness of it, a situation unfolded ahead of him, directly along the path he walked.

In a blacksmith shop down the street from Sammy, a loud crashing noise erupted in a back room, indicating items falling to the floor. In the front of the shop a slave by the name of Solomon ceased his hammering and gazed towards the loud noise; his face strained by a knowledge of the interruption's source. Immediately following the crash, a whirlwind of cursing came from the same area.

A young boy scrambled out from the back and raced to Solomon's side latching on to his leg. "Help me Pa; Mr. James is going to beat me to death!"

Solomon put his hand on his son's back. He knew there would be little he could do.

From the back room, Mr. James continued to curse and move slowly through the mess towards Solomon and his son.

Solomon took a deep breath. "You better get, boy. If anyone asks, tell them you're on an errand for Mr. James, you hear? Come to the window tonight and I'll let you in so we can talk about what to do."

At this point Mr. James had almost struggled through the mess and began to move towards the two. Solomon quickly patted his son on the back and the boy took off at full speed towards the front door.

"I'm going to beat that no good son of yours, Solomon." Mr. James then raced after the boy yelling and cursing.

At this very instant, Sammy walked in front of the large doors. Hearing the commotion he stopped and peered inside to see what had happened. He heard Mr. James yelling and then out came a young black boy, running at full speed. The boy had his head turned back. He ran straight into Sammy causing the both of them to land on the ground with a thud and dust flying up around them.

"I'm sorry, I'm sorry white boy, I didn't mean to run into you." The boy then jumped up quickly and ran off as fast as possible.

Sammy, lying on the ground, saw Mr. James coming out the door with a look of the devil on his face.

The young black boy meanwhile had made his way past the corner of a building across the street. He stopped and peeked around in the hope that Mr. James had not seen his escape route and would go the wrong way.

Sammy moved out of the man's path, but then, for some unknown reason to Sammy, as Mr. James came running out the door, he lifted his leg and tripped the man.

Mr. James had already picked up a full head of steam by the time he reached the doorway and the trip by Sammy caused him to tumble violently across the dirt street.

The young black boy saw this and burst into uncontrolled laughter. He moved back from the corner and attempted to get himself under control. He then peeked back around to watch how the situation developed.

Mr. James tumbled head over feet. Then the fury he had built up for the young black boy became refocused on the boy that tripped him. He began to swear at the boy and getting up he lunged after him.

Sammy knew now he should high tail it out of there and immediately jumped up and took off with Mr. James right behind.

Meanwhile, the young black boy followed the pursuit from a distance that kept them from being aware he was close by.

Soon enough Sammy had outrun Mr. James. Having been worn down by the fall and then the chase, Mr. James gave up and turning in frustration walked back towards the blacksmith shop, still cursing the boy's in-between trying to catch his breath.

Sammy found himself in front of a church so he sat down on the front steps to catch his breath. Soon some soldiers walked past him and into the building. Sammy glanced up at them and wondered if it was Sunday. As he caught his breath and began to relax he realized he had no idea what day of the week it actually was.

The young black boy that ran into him slowly walked up beside him. Sammy gazed into the eyes of the young boy with some apprehension and tried to determine what he wanted.

Without any words being said, he began to laugh. Sammy also began to laugh now and for a few moments both boys laughed out loud.

Several soldiers came out of the church and brushed by Sammy as they walked down the steps. He got up and motioned for the black boy to walk with him.

"I can't believe you tripped Mr. James like that. I laughed so hard."

Sammy chuckled a bit when the boy told him this.

The boy stopped and put out his hand. "My name is Benjamin. My pa calls me Ben though so I guess you can call me Ben too if you want."

Sammy shook his hand.

"I think my whole name is Samuel, but my ma calls me Sammy so you can call me Sammy."

"Nice to meet you Sammy," Ben said. The two boys smiled again and continued to walk and laugh about Mr. James falling.

Sammy now had a proud feeling inside. He couldn't remember ever feeling this way before and he liked it. He also liked this boy Ben. He couldn't remember ever actually having a friend.

A number of horse teams sped by the boys pulling cannons at high speed.

"Come on Ben; let's go through the woods so we don't get run over."

They moved off the road and walked through a wooded area. In the distance but not as far away as before, the guns and cannon rang out.

"There must be a big scrap going on over there," Sammy said as they walked.

"Yeah, I'd hate to be in the middle of that," Ben replied.

"I'm sure hungry." Sammy exclaimed wishfully.

"Me too," Ben agreed.

16

Sammy thought for a second and then continued. "I used to know where an apple tree was and it always had apples, but now days even the green ones get picked off by the grown folks."

His new friend considered what Sammy said and then got excited.

"I know where some berries might be. My pa and I had to go with some others to pick berries last summer." After Ben said this Sammy also became excited.

"Oh, berries would be great. You think you can find the spot?"

"I think so," Ben replied, gazing around to get his bearings.

"I'll follow you then." Sammy said.

The two boys walked along the side of the road as soldiers and implements of war often raced back and forth. A steady stream of civilians also struggled for space on the roads, leaving little room for the two young boys.

Keeping the road in sight they managed to make their way to an intersection which Ben remembered. Then off into the woods and across a creek. Soon they came to an open area with berry bushes.

The two ran around and began searching. A few unripe berries could be found and the boys picked these and ate them, even though they tasted very tart.

"These bushes have been picked clean," Ben said with frustration after walking all around them.

The two noticed a few berries inside the bushes, but they were beyond reach without getting stuck up by the thorns. Only the birds could get to them.

Sammy began to feel ill. His stomach had been excited at the thought of berries yet now there were few to be found. He sat down and Ben came and sat down beside him. Both boys slumped over in disappointment.

During this period of quiet self pity there came a ruckus from a corner of the small field. It seemed two birds or maybe more had become tangled up and the sound rattled the boys from their slump.

"What is that?"

"I think some birds are fighting," Ben said.

They stood up and walked over to the corner of the field and there behind a large bushy plant, remaining hidden, they spotted a single berry bush still laden with large black berries.

The birds had been fighting over them and now the boys made their way past the bushy plant that had hid them and immediately began feasting.

After a period of stuffing themselves with the juicy berries, Ben raised his head. He saw Sammy pushing berries into his mouth and the black juice had colored his lips and much of his face; this sight caused Ben to burst into laughter, spewing berries all over the place, which in turn caused Sammy to break out in laughter.

Both boys laughed until tears rolled down their cheeks. Their stomachs were full of berries and they had a great feeling after laughing so hard.

When Ben told Sammy about his face they decided to go back to the creek and wash up.

Sammy jumped in and this caused a tremendous splash. Ben, already wet after the splash, jumped in behind him.

Both of the boy's ragged clothing quickly soaked up the creek water. The extra weight became immediately noticeable but neither minded as they could only feel the joy of friendship.

The sun shone brighter and the breeze, along with the water cooled the two off. Eventually the boys got into a splashing competition and soon they'd forgotten about everything else.

Sammy splashed Ben and after dodging the water he splashed back. The sound of laughter and water play echoed throughout the area. Dragonflies danced about in the air, as if they were tiny angels, beckoning the boys to have fun.

Water ran down Sammy's face and into his eyes causing his sight to be blurred. His unruly hair, which was overdue to be cut, hung damply over his eyes, causing him to push the hair away from time to time.

Just as he was having the most fun he could remember, Sammy saw something frightening; causing him to immediately stop

18

splashing. He tried desperately to get the water and hair from his eyes in order to see.

Galloping up the creek straight towards the two of them were horses and riders. Splashes from the horses and the sun behind them caused the blurred sight to be strangely surreal to the young boy.

The mass of men and animals almost appeared to move in slow motion, but they were right on top of the boys before Ben realized anything to be amiss. The riders moved in around them as both boys stood speechless rubbing their eyes to see.

Neither one of the young boys had been this close to horses of this type before. Ben had seen horses at the blacksmith shop but few if any such as these.

The animals stood tall and trembled with energy and confidence. Several lowered their heads to drink.

Sammy glanced apprehensively up to the riders that now gazed down at the two wet boys.

They appeared to be southern soldiers, but these were much different than his friend Tommy.

Their uniforms fit better and didn't hang loosely around them. Splashes of yellow on the sleeves and collars could be seen, along with stripes of rank on a few of them. All the uniforms appeared weathered and worn though.

The soldiers expressions were of confident and well seasoned fighting men. Some had swords as well as several pistols on their belts.

One of the soldiers reached into his coat and pulled out a piece of folded paper. Another pulled his pistol out. Ben thought both would be shot right there in the creek. Neither one had enough strength to say anything. They simply stood frozen like statues.

Sammy felt his knees growing weak as he watched the man with the pistol in his hand. He then noticed the man next to him only had one arm. The other arm, or what was left of it resided in a pinned up sleeve.

Ben looked down the creek and now realized there were many more of the riders along the banks. Some gazed out over the area with rifles in hand. Others led their horses to the creek for water.

Sammy began to shiver. The day was hot but now he felt cold.

As the one soldier examined his pistol, another pulled a rifle from the case on his saddle.

All the while, the rider with the paper examined it carefully. Sammy thought this one must be the leader as he appeared to have more stuff on his uniform.

Ben wanted to move, but his legs felt as if they were locked in position.

After what seemed to be a long time the leader folded the paper up and put it into his coat. The horses' muscles twitched as they appeared ready to move again.

Sammy could smell the horses' sweat and realized he must be like a small rabbit or rodent to these magnificent animals.

The man with the pistol put it back into the holster after examining it. The man with the rifle held it on his leg as if prepared for battle.

Then the leader gazed down at Sammy and spoke. Sammy's mind had become so confused he didn't understand what the man said. Sammy said the first thing he could think of. "Wha, What?"

The man seemed irritated by this, but replied quickly.

"I said, is there a road close by?"

Sammy, realizing his arms to be still frozen in the air, simply pointed in the direction of the road.

Without saying anything the leader moved his horse towards the road and spurred it on. Then, like a train moving down the tracks, all of the riders began moving behind their leader.

The splashes, though not real high, were enough to cover the boys again with water. Some of the horses moved by so close Sammy could feel the heat of their bodies. Within a minute they had all gone as both boys stood frozen; water dripping off of them while they watched the riders disappear.

"Why didn't you tell me they were coming," Ben asked.

"I didn't know either."

Ben shook his head and both boys waded up to the bank and sat down.

"I thought for sure we'd both be shot." Ben said as they got to the bank.

"I did too, but there's no reason for them to shoot us, we ain't anybody."

Ben thought about Sammy's statement for a second.

"Well, I guess I'm a runaway slave now, so they could shoot me. And I suppose they could shoot you because you're with me."

Sammy hadn't considered this and appeared to give the situation more thought. They sat there on the bank for a while talking as their clothes dried.

The sun began to wane. "I guess we should get back," Ben finally said. "I got's to talk with my pa. He said to come to the room after dark and he'd tell me what to do."

Sammy replied with some excitement. "Hey, maybe I can come with you."

"I don't know Sammy, my pa don't like white folks. He says a white man is the reason I ain't got no ma."

Sammy considered this. He wanted to go with Ben. He didn't feel so alone while he was with his friend. Ben wanted Sammy to go with him as well but he knew his pa would be mad.

A few seconds later Sammy realized he might have the solution.

"You say your pa doesn't like white folks, but I ain't a regular white boy."

Ben looked at Sammy; puzzled by this statement.

"You ain't? What are you then?"

"I'm a bastard!"

Ben scratched his head.

"What's a bastard?"

Sammy lowered his head to his folded up knees. "I'm not fer sure, but it must be something bad. I asked my ma one time what a bastard was; she just started crying and never did tell me."

"It ain't something you can catch is it?" Ben appeared a little spooked.

"No, I don't think so, or else that mean old Terence Osbrine wouldn't have sat on me and wailed my face with his fists. That was before I knew I could outrun him though."

Both boys sat and considered the new situation. Finally, Ben decided Sammy should go with him. If his pa instructed Ben to leave Atlanta he hoped Sammy might go with him.

Chapter Three: Here's a Plan

From the cracks around the window of a small room, a dim light shined. It was crudely built and obviously attached to the back of the blacksmith shop sometime after the building had been constructed. Sammy and Ben waited at a distance from the small room. They kept an eye on the building until after dark.

"Come on." Ben said and they crept up to the room. The window they moved up to didn't have the same shape as a regular one. Sammy examined the odd rectangular window. The size of it wouldn't allow a grown person to fit through.

Ben knocked on the wooden enclosure. It opened sideways like a door and an arm came out. Ben grabbed the arm and he was then whisked up into the window out of site. Sammy stood outside waiting.

Inside the small room, Solomon pulled his son in. He then started to close the window. "Wait Pa, we need to get my friend in."

"Your friend," Solomon expressed some confusion.

"Yeah my friend, his name is Sammy."

Solomon looked outside and then reached out with an arm. Sammy took hold of the arm and also flew up and through the small window.

Once inside, Solomon stared at Sammy as if he were fishing and just pulled a large turtle into the boat. He then turned to Ben and pulled him over to the side of the room.

"What are you thinking son, bringing a white boy here. His folks will be upset that he's not home. And besides that I told you why we ain't got your ma no more. You know it was a white man that took her away."

Sammy heard everything Solomon said but he simply examined the room through the dim light of the small lamp, paying no attention to Ben's pa.

Solomon's face grimaced with anger. Ben could see the fire in his pa's eyes and felt the tight grip on his arm. He'd become familiar with this anger. His pa often talked of the white men causing his ma to be in heaven. He often talked with fire in his voice of his disregard for white folks. Ben knew he must act fast.

"But Pa, Sammy ain't a regular white boy."

Solomon glanced over at Sammy then turned back to Ben.

"What do you mean he ain't a regular white boy? He looks like a regular white boy to me."

"He ain't Pa, he's a bastard; ain't you Sammy?"

Sammy peered over at the two and nodded yes without any expression of emotion, then turned his attention back to the item hanging on the wall he'd been examining.

Ben turned back to his pa. The anger on Solomon's face appeared to melt off right in front of him. In fact, his whole face seemed to fall a bit as he gazed at the small white boy and then back at his son, which he still held by the arm.

Solomon let go of Ben. He moved slowly over to the bed and sat down behind a boot that rested upside down on a board so that the sole faced up.

"Where's your pa at boy?" he asked as he put the boot in a position between his legs in preparation to work on it.

"I ain't got a pa," Sammy replied.

"What do you mean you ain't got a pa? Everyone has a pa."

"I reckon I do, but I ain't ever met him. My ma says he's in the army. But one time I heard her tell Miss Sara she didn't rightly know who my pa was."

Solomon sat back a little, becoming more relaxed. He picked up some tools from the bed and began to work on the boot. This interested Sammy and he moved over closer to Solomon to get a better view.

"Where do you live, boy?"

Sammy gazed at the boot rather than Solomon.

"I don't rightly live anywhere. I used to stay with my Ma but she works for Madam Francine and Madam Francine don't like for me to be around anymore. I got a place to sleep under the house though. Madam Francine doesn't know about it or she'd run me off."

Solomon now expressed a keen interest in what the boy told him.

"So your ma works at Madam Francine's..., social house?"

Sammy appeared puzzled by Solomon's comment.

"I ain't ever heard it called a social house before. Terence calls it an oar house. I 'spect he don't no what he's talking about though, cause I ain't ever seen any oars in the house. That's what you use for a boat right?"

Solomon cleared his throat and went back to working on his boot. After a few seconds of thought he finally replied to the boy.

"I 'spect Terence don't know what he's talking about."

Sammy studied Solomon closely as he placed a piece of leather on the bottom of the boot.

"What cha ya doin'?"

"I'm putting a strip of leather on my boots to patch them. I put this leather back a few years ago cause I knew I'd need it. It came from a saddle I worked on and replaced pieces of the leather. The owner didn't want the old leather so I put it back for later. And now it's later and I need it on my boots."

"That's real clever," Sammy replied.

Solomon smiled, seeming happy that this boy had complimented his leather working skills.

"I'd like to learn how to do that," Sammy exclaimed cheerfully. This delighted Solomon even more and he began to show him things about leather working. Sammy in turn asked questions and helped with putting some tacks in the boots.

Ben began to take an interest now as well. He'd never realized before that his pa was so good with leather work.

After an hour of being pleasantly occupied working on his worn boots, Solomon realized it was quite late.

"Alright boys, you need to get to bed."

He gazed over at the young white boy and for the first time in a long time he didn't feel the fire in his heart towards a white person. He realized now he had been wrong to feel such a way towards all white people.

He also felt that he wanted to do something for this young boy that was not much better off than he and Ben. He thought for a second, and then made a decision.

"Sammy, I've got something here you might like to have."

Solomon reached up on a small shelf and pulled a shiny little metal item down.

"This is a leather punch." He handed the worn piece of metal to Sammy. "I just keep it around for a spare anymore as it's fairly worn out. But since you like working with leather, it might help you get started."

Sammy's eyes lit up as he gazed upon the small punch. The metal felt warm and a little heavy in his hand. Ben watched on and also felt happy that his pa had taken a shine to Sammy.

"Thank you Mr. Ben's Pa." Sammy smiled as he gazed at the small metal punch in his hand.

"Alright," Solomon said with a chuckle. "You can stay here tonight, but you boys got to get gone before daylight and before Mr. James shows up."

Then Solomon called Ben over to him. "Listen son," he said quietly, "the Yankees will be here any day now. I keep hearing the folks say the Reb's can't hold them back. You got to leave here bright and early, before Mr. James comes. You stay around until the Yankees get here and then come and find me alright."

"Alright Pa, I will."

Solomon continued. "After the Yankees get here the white folks won't be able to keep slaves anymore and Mr. James can't keep us. We'll go away from here."

"Can Sammy come with us, Pa?"

Solomon peered over at the boy lying on a ragged blanket in the corner.

"Well, he has his ma here and I'm sure she would miss him. You just do as I say and we can make better plans later. You got it, Son?"

"Yeah Pa, I understand."

The man thought of the two boys as Ben went and lay down in his usual spot on the floor. He wondered why grown people couldn't be more like children.

Solomon slept very little that night and when he did sleep it was lightly. Finally daylight could be seen making its way closer to the horizon. Solomon knew he must get the boys away before Mr. James arrived.

"Get up. You two need to go now." Solomon nudged the two boys. "Come on, you two got to get gone before Mr. James gets here." They rubbed their eyes as Solomon opened the small window. He then hoisted them out one by one. "Remember what I said Ben."

"Alright Pa, I will." They set off through the streets of Atlanta. The gunfire could be heard already on the edge of the city. As they wandered around town with no place to go, the cannon shot landed randomly in the streets.

"I'm so hungry I can't stand it," Sammy blurted out. Ben agreed with this sentiment.

"You think there are more berries?" Sammy asked as he held his stomach.

"Maybe," his friend replied as if in thought about it. "I guess we can go see."

"Yeah, I could sure eat some right now." Sammy could almost taste the berries as he thought about them. The two quickly headed back to the berry patch.

Upon arriving at the patch they found the berries had been consumed by the birds for the most part. A few stragglers took the edge off the boys' hunger pains yet fell far from filling their empty stomachs.

As they moved back across the creek Sammy spotted something moving on the bank. He ran over and picked up a small green turtle. Ben quickly came alongside to examine the find. The little turtle moved its legs in mid air as if trying to walk. The boys laughed about this and for a few minutes forgot about their hunger.

"I'm going to name him Snapper," Sammy said.

"That's a good name, but he ain't snapping at you."

"I know he ain't, but the name sounds like he might and if someone wants to hold him they'll think he might snap at them."

"Yeah, that's a good idea," Ben said as he touched Snapper on the head.

"I want to show Snapper to my Ma,"

"Maybe she has something we could eat," Ben added with an eager expression.

"Yeah, maybe, But she don't eat much anymore. She just drinks from her big bottle and takes her medicine a lot. She might know where we can get something to eat though. I'll ask her. We got to be quiet going in though. If Madam Francine catches us we'll get thrown out by our ears."

"I'll follow you then," Ben replied.

The two moved back into the city and dodging soldiers and civilians finally arrived at Madam Francine's.

As they approached the large two story house a wagon could be seen in the front; women were being helped into it by several men.

Sammy and Ben crept up behind the house and into the back door. Once inside, Sammy led Ben to one of his hiding spots.

Madam Francine and Sara seemed to be the only people still in the house and they busily put things in several large bags.

When the two ladies had gone into other rooms Sammy took hold of Ben's arm and away they went up the stairs. Sammy knocked on his mother's door lightly as usual.

Inside the room his mother awoke to the knock. Her first thought was that a man had arrived for her services. Elsa pulled herself out of the bed. Stumbling around her small dresser she found a tiny bottle. Opening the bottle she put her finger over the top and put the remainder of the contents on her neck.

Gazing into the small glass container she realized nothing now remained inside. She moaned with disappointment about this as she tried to run her fingers through her messy hair and arrange it better. As she looked around the room for a comb the door opened slightly.

"Ma," Sammy called inside the door as he opened it a little more.

"Oh, Sammy, I thought you was, well somebody else." She then sat on the bed and fell back on it as if exhausted.

"Ma, I wanted to show you something. And I want you to meet my friend."

His mother mumbled something under her breath. Ben came into the room behind Sammy and shut the door.

"Ma, where is everybody?"

His mother again acted as if she were only half awake as she mumbled sleepily.

"Where are they, Ma?"

"I don't know Sammy, maybe they went to a ball or a picnic," she replied, seeming a bit frustrated with her son.

"I just wondered," the boy said meekly. Sammy crawled onto the bed and pulled Snapper from his pocket.

"Look Ma this is my new pet. His name is Snapper, but he doesn't really snap at you." He held the turtle over her face.

"Oh, take that away from me, please." She waved her hand, trying to push the turtle away without touching it.

Sammy laughed and Ben laughed also.

"Who's that Sammy?"

"That's my friend Ma, the one I told you I wanted you to meet."

His mother groaned in a questioning manner and then with what appeared to be much effort, sat up on the edge of the bed. Upon seeing Ben, she sat back a little and raised her head in surprise.

"Well, it's a... He's a little black boy!"

"Yeah Ma, this is Ben, my friend." Sammy replied with joy.

"Well, Sammy, where are all of your little white friends?"

The young boy stared at his mother with a puzzled expression. Then, slowly realizing she wasn't at all aware of the situation, his head lowered a bit as he responded.

"I ain't got any other friends, Ma."

His mother gazed over at her son and an obvious expression of pain came to her face. She suddenly realized how little she knew of Sammy's daily life. She didn't want to see it, but here it was directly in front of her.

She tried hard to be a mother now, even though she was harshly aware that she knew so little about being one.

Although it wasn't common for a white boy and a black boy to be considered friends, she knew she'd not been a friend or a mother to Sammy. Elsa swallowed her pride and tried hard to do the right thing now.

"Oh, well, I see." She then looked back at Ben. "Well, it's nice to meet you then, Ben."

Ben smiled at Elsa.

"You sure smell pretty Mrs. Sammy's Ma."

She smiled back when he said this. Ben continued,

"I think you must smell like an angel. My Pa says my Ma is an angel up in heaven. I think she probably smells pretty just like you."

Sammy's mother almost began to cry and seemed to labor to keep from breaking down in tears. She raised her hand and ran it along Ben's cheek.

"My goodness, you're certainly the little gentleman. I don't believe I've ever had anyone say such a nice thing to me."

Sammy now came over and sat beside his mother. He felt a little sad that he'd never thought to say anything that nice to his mother.

Elsa realized she still had the small, empty perfume bottle in her hand. She looked at it and then held her hand out to Ben.

"Here you go Ben. This is for giving me such a nice compliment."

Ben took the tiny bottle and peered down at it with delight. The tiny glass container was still warm from being in Elsa's hand. It glimmered and shined. He'd never owned anything this nice before. It seemed like a little treasure to him and he put it in his pocket quickly so he wouldn't lose it.

Elsa put her arm around Sammy. "Well you know what they say Sammy."

"What do they say, Ma?"

"I've heard it said that one good friend is better than ten fair weather friends." She then hugged Sammy and he smiled. She also rubbed Ben's head and all three smiled.

"Ma, we're real hungry. You have anything to eat?"

The smile melted from Elsa's face as she considered this situation. She then fell backwards, moaning as the responsibilities of being a mother fell harshly upon her once again.

"No I don't have anything. Go ask Sara to get you something." She then moved herself back onto the bed and rolled over into what appeared to be her favorite position to sleep.

Sammy's heart sank a bit as he knew there would be no use to ask Sara for anything.

Ben looked at his friend with a confused expression. Sammy then shrugged his shoulders indicating he didn't know what to do. After a few moments Sammy waved to Ben that they should leave.

He glanced out the door to make sure no one would see them. Then they crept out and down the stairs. When the two boys reached the first floor Sammy realized the entire house had become silent. He quietly moved into the parlor and no one stirred. He then walked around to other parts of the house with Ben following behind. The house didn't have a soul inside other than his mother, himself and Ben.

"Where is everyone?" Ben asked in a hushed voice.

"I don't know," Sammy replied, seeming just as confused as Ben. They moved cautiously to the kitchen and searched in vain for something to eat. Morning crept closer to noon and the boys had only eaten a few berries. Finding no food anywhere they headed to the door.

As they tried to go out the back, Sammy found the door to be locked. The boys then went to the front door and found this one locked also. Finally Sammy located a window to make an escape from and they both slipped out of the large house.

Chapter Four: The Storm

Strolling down the streets, the boys began to notice that most businesses were closed.

"You think today is Sunday? Sammy asked as they moved down the strangely vacant streets.

"I don't know what today is, but I ain't heard any church bells."

Sammy pulled Snapper out of his pocket and they walked along, talking to the small turtle and paying little attention to the increased cannon and rifle fire. Then Sammy stopped.

"Hey, I know what we can do. We can go see my friend Tommy."

"Who's Tommy?" Ben asked.

"He's a soldier and he's got some biscuits called hardtack. They don't taste so great and they're real hard, but I'd eat about as many as I could get right now." Just as they spoke about this, a large mortar shell made a whoosh, whoosh, whoosh sound as it passed menacingly overhead.

"That one's going to hit close," Sammy said, just about the time it landed in the distance with a crash. The boys gazed in the direction of the explosion for a few seconds. Then Sammy turned his attention back to Snapper and this in turn caused Ben to also look at the little turtle.

"Come on, I'll bet Tommy will like Snapper." Sammy put the turtle in his pocket.

They darted off in the direction of Tommy's guard post. Sammy led Ben through the wooded area until they reached the edge of the small field.

"The fighting sure sounds close by," Ben commented nervously as the gunfire now seemed even closer. Sammy noticed this as well but the thought of the hardtack had a hold on him.

"Yeah, it's kind of close, but it moves around. It'll move off shortly I figure; come on he's just over in that big hole yonder." With that Sammy darted across the small field with Ben running behind, trying to keep up.

"It's me Tommy, don't shoot," Sammy yelled out right before jumping into trench. He bound over the dirt mound and slid down into the earthworks. Ben came sliding down behind him. Once the dust settled, the boys surveyed the entrenchment. Tommy lay motionless against the dirt wall, as if asleep. The two boys stared at his back.

"Tommy, you awake? It's me Sammy."

The young soldier didn't respond.

"Is he asleep?" Ben asked, obviously becoming nervous about the situation. Sammy moved slowly over to where Tommy lay.

"Tommy... Are you asleep, Tommy?" As the young boy moved around to Tommy's face, his body cringed inside and his small empty stomach turned with a nauseous repulsion. Tommy stared off into space with a blank stare. Square in his forehead a large bullet hole marked the end of the young man's life. Sammy's face became contorted as he'd never been this close to a dead person, particularly someone he had known.

"What's wrong?" Ben asked as he knew something to be amiss.

"He's, dead," was all Sammy could utter.

"He's dead?" Ben's voice cracked with fright.

"We got's to get out of here Sammy. Who ever kill't him might still be around." Ben glanced around nervously.

"Yeah, I guess you're right." Sammy moved towards Ben, but stopped. "Wait," he said as if remembering something.

"Wait for what?"

Sammy moved back over to the young soldier's body. He gently reached into the pocket he'd seen Tommy get the hardtack from and pulled out the folded cloth. He moved back to where Ben sat and unfolded the cloth displaying several small pieces of hardtack.

"What are you doing Sammy? That's a dead man's food, we can't eat that."

"Why not," Sammy asked as he stared down at the hard biscuits in the cloth.

"I told you, it belongs to a dead man."

"So, he doesn't need it anymore."

Ben now gazed down at the small fragments of food in Sammy's hand.

"What does it matter, Ben; we're either goina get shot or die of hunger. If I get shot to death, at least I don't want to be hungry."

Ben glanced at Sammy and back at the hardtack. What his friend said did seem to make sense.

"Alright, I guess that's the truth of the matter," he said and both of them gingerly took a small piece and started chewing on the hard biscuits.

As they discussed this and nibbled on the hardtack, the two boys seemed unaware of the war creeping in all around them. Sammy pulled Snapper from his pocket.

"I wonder if Snapper will eat hardtack." He held a small piece in front of the turtle.

"He ain't goina eat it," Ben said with a smile and watching the turtle. When Snapper showed no interest, Sammy put the piece of hardtack in his own mouth and chewed on it.

"Hey, look there!" Sammy jumped down and grabbed a small bug that was crawling in the dirt. "He'll eat this I'll bet you." He held the bug up to Snapper's mouth. After looking at the bug closely, Snapper reached out and slowly bit the head off the small insect.

"Oh, I told you he would!" Sammy exclaimed with a chuckle, and moved the insect's body a little closer so the turtle could get another bite.

As the two boys were waiting for the turtle to take another bite, a soldier in a blue uniform came over the dirt mound with a force that stirred up a dusty haze in the trench.

The shock to the boys was tremendous as dirt flew about and the man landed with rifle and bayonet ready to run someone through.

He had a beard and a blue cap that matched his uniform. First he pointed the musket with bayonet towards Tommy but seeing he was already dead he immediately aimed it at Sammy and Ben. Both boys' heart skipped a beat as they thought again they were surely dead.

The soldier examined the two boys nervously, moving the musket from one to the other. Sammy held Snapper in one hand and the dead bug in the other. Ben sat with a piece of hardtack halfway to his mouth. Both boys' eyes were frozen in fright.

The soldier in blue appeared to be confused at the sight he beheld. Then, after he realized the boys posed no danger, he put the butt of his musket on the ground and proceeded to reload it. All the while he kept watching the two boys, as if he were still not completely sure of their intentions.

The Yankee hurriedly put the powder and shot into the barrel. Then pulled a long rod out from a holder in the musket and tamped everything down. He then quickly lifted it up and put a cap onto the hammer mechanism. The boys watched this procedure without moving a muscle.

When the soldier finished, he nodded at the boys and began climbing out of the earthworks. As he reached the top and stood up, a shot rang out. The soldier flew backwards into the trench landing face up in front of the boys.

They looked down at him with eyes still wide. He stared straight into space with a bullet hole in his forehead similar to the one Tommy had. Blood flowed from the wound as the boys now stared straight into the soldier's face of death.

A rider in a grayish brown uniform rode up to the trench with pistol drawn and pointed it at the boys. He looked at Sammy and Ben. As his horse moved nervously under him, he turned his head slightly in confusion at what he saw, while still pointing his pistol at them. Then, as it appeared to register that he was in fact looking at two young boys, he spurred his horse and rode off.

The sounds of war now rang loudly in the boys' ears. Everything came into perspective and they suddenly realized the war wasn't somewhere else, but right on top of them.

"We've got to get out of here Sammy!" Ben now spoke with panic in his voice.

"Yeah, let's go," Sammy said as he gazed back in shock at the dead soldier lying at his feet.

They crawled to the top of the trench and peered out. Chaos had overtaken the area and all around them soldiers moved about to and fro. Soldiers on horses appeared to have some control of the area. Moving about at a rapid gallop they shot at the many soldiers in blue.

"Come on Ben let's get out of here."

"No wait," Ben replied, seeming reluctant to leave the security of the trench.

"I'm not waiting Ben, let's go!" And with that the boys took off across the short open area in route to the woods.

Cannon shot landed not far from them and bullets whizzed by like bees close to their head. Several of the riders noticed them, but realized they were only young boys and retracted from gunning them down.

After stumbling several times and getting back up the two made their frantic escape to the wooded area.

Once they reached the woods, the winded boys collapsed onto the ground. Both lay in the brush, frightened, exhausted and trying to catch their breath. In the trees above projectiles cut through branches. A small branch landed on Sammy and with this they began crawling on the ground in another desperate effort to get away from the battlefield.

The sounds of war began to fade some as they moved farther away; the boys stood up and ran as fast as they could. On the road were injured and bloodied soldiers moving towards Atlanta.

Wagons with large crosses on the sides moved rapidly along with various implements of war, all struggling for a piece of the narrow road.

When they reached the edge of town smoke billowed all around the city and mortar shells exploded in buildings and houses. The boys moved slowly and desperately, trying to avoid the chaotic action all around them.

Meanwhile, across town at the blacksmith shop, Mr. James began gathering tools together and packed belongings.

"We're getting out of Atlanta while we still can Solomon; grab those tongs and that bag there."

Solomon was stunned by this new development.

"Where is it we're going to, Mr. James?"

"Away from here, come on get those things together!"

Solomon moved slowly. A mortar shell landed close by and both men stopped and gazed out the door in the direction of its impact.

"Come on Solomon, before one of those things lands on top of us." Mr. James now shouted with frustration.

Solomon gathered the items together but moved as slow as he could. He glanced around hoping that Ben might be close enough for him to get his attention. Then he considered running off himself.

Many different thoughts ran through his mind now that the situation had changed. He'd never considered Mr. James leaving his blacksmith shop when he told Ben to stay away.

After a while Mr. James seemed to decide he'd gathered all the items he and Solomon could carry. They moved outside and he quickly locked the doors on the shop.

"Let's go Solomon."

The large black man gazed around with reluctance and moved very slowly.

"Come on, let's go," Mr. James' voice became louder.

"We've got to wait for Benjamin," Solomon now began searching frantically for his son.

"We're not waiting around, we're going. Grab that stuff and let's go; we'll worry about that worthless boy later."

"I'm not leaving my son!" Solomon's voice expressed anger as the gunfire and battle noises echoed not far in the distance.

Then a large explosion shook the ground and everything around them. Mr. James appeared quite unnerved by this event.

"The Yankees will be here anytime now, you better get moving Solomon, I ain't staying around here any longer."

Solomon, becoming quite frantic himself, now went straight up to Mr. James face and boldly declared, "I'm not leaving without Benjamin!"

Mr. James slapped Solomon across his face.

The large black man cocked his arm back and immediately hit Mr. James square in the face, causing him to fall backwards. He then turned around and began walking away.

"Ben... Benjamin, where are you," he called loudly as he moved quickly away from Mr. James.

Mr. James put his hand up to his mouth and then lowered it to see blood. He cursed at Solomon. He pulled a pistol from under his coat, aimed it at Solomon's back and fired three shots in rapid succession.

Solomon fell to the ground.

Mr. James stared at the man lying on the ground. He again put his hand to his mouth as if trying to justify killing Solomon.

Then, a familiar and ominous sound could be heard falling from the sky. Mr. James looked up in horror.

As if judgment were being called upon him for the murder he'd just committed, he watched the slow moving shell falling almost squarely upon him. It landed in the middle of the blacksmith shop, immediately killing him as well as covering his body and Solomon's with debris.

Only Solomon's worn shoes could be seen from under the wooden shards of the shattered building.

The fighting reached a fever pitch as the Rebels hastily retreated and the Yankees began taking over the battered city. The two young boys moved desperately and almost unnoticed back into the edge of Atlanta.

Chaos reigned as Rebel soldiers seemed to be everywhere and moving quickly as if to get away from something.

Sammy and Ben walked cautiously into Atlanta. A large explosion followed by smaller ones rocked the ground. Smoke floated everywhere and the city appeared to be coming apart.

As they fearfully maneuvered themselves through the streets, trying to grasp the situation, the completely unexpected happened; they ran almost square into Terence Osbrine and several of his rough buddies.

Before Sammy had the chance to make a run for it Terence held him by the collar of his shirt.

Realizing these were not good boys, Ben backed away and to the edge of the closest building.

"Let me go!" Sammy protested and tried to pull loose.

"What are you doin' ya little bastard? Are you traveling with a runaway slave now?" Terence may not have been very smart but he had a keen eye for a person's weakness.

Sammy knew he should come up with something in a hurry.

"He ain't any runaway, and if you don't let us do the errands Mr. James told us to do, then he'll for sure get you."

Terence didn't appear to be worried by Sammy's claim, but the remark did cause him to slow down and think a bit. After a few seconds he let Sammy go, but as he did so, pushed him down in the middle of the street.

"It's just lucky for you we're on our way to join up with the army. They say if you look sixteen they'll let you join now and we're on our way to be soldiers."

As Sammy lay on the ground the boys laughed and began walking off. Sammy waited until they were a safe distance away before saying anything.

He then stood up in the middle of the street; he also happened to be standing in the center of an intersection.

Sammy yelled out defiantly. "Yeah, ya'll go ahead and do that."

Ben moved around the corner of the building.

"Come on Sammy let's just go, "he said in a lowered voice.

Sammy glanced at Ben. "I ain't afraid of them skunks." He then turned back towards Terence, but before he could say anything else he noticed a wagon heading towards him at a fast pace.

The young boy stepped back and out of the way. He then yelled out again.

"Ya'll go ahead and join up; go right ahead and get yourselves killed like my friend Tommy."

As he said this, something fell whistling from the sky and in front of Terence and the other boys. Sammy barely got a glimpse of the object, but when it hit in front of them a wave of dirt spewed from the ground.

Then the object bounced up and at this very instant the wagon moved between Sammy and the rough boys.

A white light went off and everything went black for Sammy.

Ben had moved back around the building after asking Sammy to ignore Terence and the other boys. He didn't want any problems now as he remembered his pa telling him to come back to the blacksmith shop when the Yankees arrived.

He heard Sammy tell them something about getting killed like his friend Tommy. Then an explosion almost knocked him to the ground. Debris flew from the corner of the building.

Ben's ears rang due to the close proximity of the mortar shell. When he regained his composure he thought for certain Sammy must be lying on the other side of the building dead.

Still in shock from the blast and with his ears painfully ringing, Ben peeked around the corner to see smoke along with wreckage all around, presenting a hellish picture. He saw no sign of Sammy. The wagon appeared to have caught most of the blast from the mortar shell.

The contents of the wagon lay spread out in the street. Cloth and clothing of all sorts along with pieces of the wagon and various remnants of furniture lay disbursed in the street where Sammy had last been seen.

There appeared to be nothing left of Terence and the other boys. Ben looked over to the location where they stood and this appeared to be the point of impact, or very close to it.

Sammy opened his eyes to see white in front of him. He couldn't remember who or where he was. His ears rang loudly. Slowly he began to remember a few things. He began to remember who he was. He wondered why he could only see white. He also wondered why he felt hot.

Gradually, he began to remember him and Ben walking along the streets. After a few more minutes he could remember yelling at Terence and the strange object falling from the sky in front them. He must be dead he thought to himself. A mortar shell must have landed on all of them and now he's dead.

The young boy considered the sensation of being dead. Strange, he thought; there's only a ringing sound when one is dead. He thought there would be singing and such.

Then he tried moving. He felt as though something held him down. With some effort he raised his arm and pointed up. He could see his hand but something was lying on top of him.

Ben yelled out for Sammy. He walked around the rubble that had once been the wagon. He grimaced and felt ill as he saw body parts from the driver lying about. He turned away and tried to find something else to look at.

He examined the mule or horse; he wasn't sure which it was as it also lay torn apart in the street.

"Sammy...Sammy where are you?" The boy concluded Sammy must have been blown into nothing just as Terence and the others. Then, he noticed something poking up from under some white cloth.

"Sammy, is that you?" He ran over and quickly pulled the cloth off of Sammy. His friend appeared dazed and pointing his arm straight out as if pointing at something. Ben looked but didn't see anything in the sky where Sammy pointed. It didn't matter though as he was so happy his friend was still alive.

"Are you alright?"

Sammy continued to point up into the sky. He had a strange blank expression on his face and made no reply to Ben.

Ben pulled him over by the building and into the shade. It seemed to be around noon now and Ben sat in the thin shade of the building with Sammy, not knowing what to do.

Sammy finally lowered his arm and slept for a little while.

After an hour or so Ben became aware of a strange silence. He still heard some gunfire in the distance but not around him as before. The sounds of mortar shells hitting the city had stopped. The streets also became oddly inactive.

He sat with Sammy, watching for any sign of people, but as the minutes slipped by there seemed to be no one around.

Finally, several streets down from them, soldiers on horses could be seen riding quickly to and fro. Some had rifles drawn and others had a pistol in their hand. He couldn't tell what color uniform they wore but he thought it might be blue.

He also heard other riders behind him somewhere, but wasn't able to see those.

Though Ben didn't know for certain about the soldiers, they did in fact wear blue uniforms. The Union cavalry rode quickly but cautiously as they entered the outer parts of Atlanta. The Confederates had begun pulling out and these soldiers were not far from their heels.

A Yankee cavalry unit that had a reputation for fighting hard, drinking hard, and womanizing whenever possible rode into the outskirts of Atlanta. They kept an eye out for Rebel troops, but they also kept an eye out for abandon establishments that may have any type of drinking alcohol inside.

When a lieutenant saw Madam Francine's he rode up to the door and jumped down from his horse. Several of his men filed in behind him.

They checked the front door to find it locked. One of the men kicked the door open and after peering inside carefully, moved in and began rummaging around with caution.

Several of the soldiers broke into a locked cabinet and found a small amount of whiskey and other assorted half full bottles. This sparked a renewed effort to search the entire house. Soon a number of their fellow soldiers arrived. One of them went up stairs and began searching the rooms. He opened the door of Elsa's room and saw her asleep on the bed.

"Hey, there's still a whore up here in this room!" All the soldiers downstairs stopped and stared up at him. Then they began running up the stairs. Elsa, now hearing the ruckus woke up to find several Union soldiers staring in at her.

"What are you doing here? Get out of my room," she said with a weak voice.

The lieutenant ran up the stairs and pushed the men aside. He got to the door and looked in at Elsa.

"The rest of you are going to have to wait your turn, according to rank." He then went in and closed the door. Elsa screamed, but after several slaps were heard the screams stopped. The other soldiers laughed about this and continued to search the house as they awaited their turn.

Several hours and many soldiers later, a man with a callous appearance stared down at Elsa with an expression of guilt. He lifted her lifeless arm as if to check his suspicion. Seeing that she had no life left in her, he gazed around, to make sure no one else was aware he'd abused the woman to the point of death. He crept out of the room as he pulled his blue uniform back on; then slipped down the stairs to join the rest of his unit, which had already begun to move into the city.

Meanwhile, Sammy slowly recovered by the side of the building. He still had trouble hearing Ben speak and asked him to repeat what he said several times. The ringing in his ears gradually subsided and his hearing returned.

Ben found a cup from the wagon wreckage and got Sammy a drink of water from somewhere. Then Sammy remembered Snapper.

He reached into the pocket where he kept the little pet and pulled it out. The tiny turtle hadn't survived the blast.

Sammy and Ben stared with sadness at the dead turtle for several minutes, not knowing what to do.

"I guess we should bury him," Sammy finally said with a tear welling in his eye and as several more riders in blue galloped noisily by. The two boys piled some dirt from the street on top of Snapper, holding their tiny funeral as more and more Union troops began to move past.

Sammy found a piece of wood and stuck it in the small mound as a makeshift marker.

The day had worn down and as the sun began to set the two weary boys starred at the tiny grave in silence.

Chapter Five: The Remnants

"The Yankees are everywhere now ain't they," Sammy remarked as the two began to take notice of their surroundings again.

"Yeah, I guess I can go back to my Pa now. He said to come back after the Yankees got here."

Sammy considered what he should do. He still had a lost feeling due to the day's events. Finally, he thought of the place he considered his home.

"I think I should go check on Ma," He said weakly, seeming still disoriented.

Both of the boys were tired and hungry, yet they sat for several minutes, resisting the effort of leaving each other's company. With some reluctance the two separated as dusk settled in.

After a long and cautious walk through the much quieter streets of Atlanta, Ben approached the blacksmith shop. He immediately realized something wasn't right. Where the building had sat before he could see only wreckage.

His movement slowed. His eyes searched frantically for his father. Maybe, he stood close by waiting for Ben to run into his arms. Maybe mean old Mr. James had been caught in the explosion and he and his pa could leave now. Ben sifted his mind for any answer other than the fear he now began to feel.

"Pa, are you here Pa?" He began nervously climbing through the boards and debris.

"Pa... Pa...." He now became more certain something very bad had happened to his father. His every step grew weaker as the possible reality took hold of him.

Then, he saw something familiar sticking out from under mangled boards. His pa's boot could be seen. The leather he had replaced the night before now faced the young boy as unmistakable proof of what he feared.

"Pa...." Ben almost fell over as he called to his father weakly. He sat down on the debris and stared at the boot in dismay. Tears began to stream down his cheeks. Dark crept over the city and the smell of burning wood accented the misery Ben found himself in. He became lost within himself and grief as the night took over.

The young boy remained by the lifeless body of his father throughout the night. He could only cry until sleep briefly came and went as a temporary reprieve from sorrow.

On another side of Atlanta, Sammy had reached Madam Francine's before darkness settled in and found the doors wide open.

The sensation of walking up the front steps felt foreign to the young boy as he had no memory of ever going into the house this way.

He cautiously moved his head into the broken doorway and viewed the mass of wrecked furniture, along with numerous other household items, all strewn about in disarray.

Sammy wondered what event would cause such a thing. Stepping around the mess he cautiously moved through the house and up the stairs. He opened the door to his mother's room and peeked in to see her laying face down on the bed. He felt better seeing her there as he'd become worried due to all the chaos downstairs.

"Ma... Ma.... What happen to the house, Ma?" Sammy moved up to the bed. "Ma, are you asleep?" His mother didn't move. Now the familiar feeling that always scared him returned. He started to touch her arm but stopped. He was afraid now. Somehow inside he knew what he feared to be true, but he didn't want to confirm it.

Maybe if he didn't touch her he could pretend everything would be alright. He continued to stare at her, not wanting to know. Then he slowly realized that he had to know. He realized he could do nothing if he didn't know.

Maybe she just slept as before and all this concern would be for nothing. He slowly reached down and touched her arm. She was cold. He pulled his hand back. Tears began to well up and fall involuntarily from his eyes. He suddenly felt more alone than he'd ever felt before.

The light in the room faded and darkness overtook the young boy. His body weighed him down; he felt old and tired. He slowly crawled into his mother's bed and snuggled up to her lifeless body as he wept with very little sound, only tears.

He nuzzled her brown hair. He could still smell her. He'd never really thought about how his mother smelled until Ben had said something. He wanted to remember how his mother smelled.

The result of his weeping fell into his mother's hair and Sammy continued to cry until he faded off into a grieving sleep.

As the following morning broke, Sammy reluctantly left his mother and wandered in a daze to the street. He walked for a while as soldiers in blue rode past him. He turned a corner and met more soldiers in blue marching towards him. He moved out of the way and stood by a few moments gazing along the long column of blue uniforms.

He didn't know what to do or where to go. Then he thought of Ben. He made his way across town as the morning sunlight splashed onto the vacant buildings of the city.

As he stumbled to where the blacksmith shop had been, he spotted Ben sitting in the midst of the debris.

Sammy staggered across the broken boards and up to his friend. Ben turned to Sammy. When he saw him he immediately began to cry again.

"Pa's... dead, Sammy."

Sammy looked at the boot underneath the rubble. He felt sad but couldn't cry anymore. He slumped down beside his friend. Ben continued to weep, but having Sammy beside him made him feel better.

"My Ma's dead too," Sammy finally said with defeat in his voice.

Ben looked at Sammy with an expression of shock. He then turned back to where his father lay.

Somehow this made him feel better. He didn't like that, and inside he was a little upset with himself for feeling this way. Still, he didn't feel as alone now. It seemed that somehow Sammy and he would find a way to survive. If he were by himself, Ben didn't think he would make it.

The sun began to beat down on the boys.

"Come on Ben, we can't stay here."

They climbed out of the wrecked building and began walking wearily down the streets. Neither had eaten since the previous morning.

Stumbling around aimlessly, the two were almost ran over several times by army wagons. Smoke drifted around the streets. Union soldiers were now entering the city in mass.

Finally, neither Ben nor Sammy could walk any farther. They sat down in the shade by a building. The soldiers marched by, stopping at times, and then they would start moving again.

Methodical sounds and movements of the entering army lulled the two boys as if in some type of rocking chair. By afternoon the exhausted and hungry boys were leaned against each other, fast asleep.

The warm day seemed to linger endlessly as the entering troops moved and stopped, moved and stopped. Eventually, some of the many tradesmen that followed the army came through town, following the army units they were associated with.

One of the wagons creeping through the now muted city happened to stop beside where Sammy and Ben huddled against the building. In the wagon a woman sat beside her husband as he held the reins of the horse team.

The woman gazed down as they waited to move again and saw what she initially thought to be a pile of rags beside the structure. Her heart cried out inside her chest when she realized this to be two boys leaning against each other and seemingly asleep.

Then she became frightened as a thought came to her; maybe they were dead. She grabbed her husband's arm to bring his attention to the boys and then climbed down from the wagon.

"Are you boys alright?"

Ben woke up first and gazed into the woman's face. He simply looked at her as he wasn't sure what to say. Sammy then woke up.

"Are you two alright?" She knelt down beside the boys.

"Where are your parents?"

"We ain't got no parents," Sammy replied.

"So you're orphans?"

"What does that mean?" Ben asked weakly.

The woman smiled a little, but in a sad way. "Well, it means your parents are either dead or missing."

"I think that's what we are cause our parents are dead," Sammy replied dolefully.

The woman's face grimaced as if in pain after hearing this. She turned and peered at the man in the wagon. He said nothing but his face also expressed compassion.

"Would you boys like to come with us for a bit? We could give you something to eat, at least."

Sammy turned to Ben and his friend had an expression indicating he was ready to do anything to get away from the road.

"Yeah, that would be good," Sammy replied and they stood up. The woman helped the two into the wagon and not long after she had reseated herself the army began to move again.

As the day came to a close the wagon stopped and they made camp on the southeastern edge of Atlanta.

The woman told the boys her name was Mary, and her husband's name was Nathaniel but she called him Nate.

Mary cooked a wonderful supper over a fire. Neither one of the boys could remember eating such a grand meal and both ate until they were almost sick.

After the meal, Mary found several of Nate's old nightshirts. The thought of how they would likely swallow the boys up caused her to laugh a little. She made a small bath for them and had them clean up. After bathing, each one put a nightshirt on.

Mary washed their clothes, being careful not to lose anything. The tattered clothing was then hung up to dry and they all sat around the small campfire.

"Nate and I never actually intended to follow the army," she explained. "Nate does leather work and I'm a seamstress. We took work on from the soldiers and officers. Then the army began to move."

"We'll move with the army for a ways, we thought, so we can get these jobs finished. Then other jobs came in and we moved a little farther. Before we knew it, we were so far south we couldn't do anything other than stay with the army. So now, we've got to stay close to the troops until we get to a safe place."

She stared into the fire as it crackled and a few embers floated effortlessly up into the night sky.

"It's not so bad though. We're earning good money as there's always work. We just have to stay far enough back to keep out of the fighting, but close enough we don't find ourselves alone in unfriendly territory."

Nate puffed on his pipe and nodded every once in a while.

The boys continued to stay with Mary and Nate. Sammy began to learn about leather craft and Ben found a mother figure in Mary.

As time went by, Nate and Mary sat the boys down to talk with them.

"Nate and I have been discussing the situation boys."

Ben and Sammy looked at each other. Both were immediately worried they wouldn't be able to stay with the couple any longer.

"We've decided that if you boys wish to stay with us, we would like for you to stay as long as you want."

When Mary said this both boys smiled with joy. They could barely sit still. Mary continued.

"The army will move again, once the weather begins to warm back up. And this isn't an easy life. But when the war is over we'll go back to Pennsylvania and have a real home."

Ben and Sammy both loved their new adoptive parents very much and tried hard to do work and earn their keep. They also continued to become as brothers to each other. The experiences that had broken their meager homes had also bonded the two together.

Months later, as spring flowers began to boom, the army packed up and began moving south again. The two boys once again sat in the back of the wagon as it moved slowly down the road.

Soon a wall of smoke was seen rising behind them. Everyone became bewildered by this. As a cavalry officer on horseback rode around the wagon Nate yelled out to him.

"What's all the smoke from, Lieutenant?"

The officer slowed his horse down and briefly moved along side the wagon.

"Atlanta is burning to the ground. Soon there won't be anything left but a memory."He then waved slightly and spurring his horse galloped ahead.

When Sammy and Ben heard this they looked at each other with sadness. Then, both gazed back towards the only homes they had known. The wagon jostled the boys about as it took them farther and farther from Atlanta.

After a few quiet moments, Ben seemed to remember something. He reached into his pocket and pulled the tiny perfume bottle out. He examined the item carefully. It had become very dear to him and he always kept it safely in his pocket.

Sammy, seeing Ben do this, reached into his own pocket and pulled out the small leather punch. He studied the worn metal item in his hand.

They both examined the objects as if trying to pull something that had been lost from them.

Then, without saying anything, Ben moved his hand slowly over to Sammy, indicating he wanted to give the tiny bottle to his friend.

Sammy gazed down at the small bottle, and then he glanced at the leather punch in his own hand. Sammy slowly moved his hand with the leather punch over to Ben.

Sammy took the bottle and Ben took the leather punch. They both smiled softly to each other. Then the two boys turned, and each holding their new treasure, watched the smoke rising from Atlanta until it was a distant sight.

The End

Twelve Minutes till Midnight

Gray Door Ltd.

54

The Days of Reckoning

A swarm of cicadas filled the warm day of May 1934 with their chorus of screeching songs. Suddenly, the insects halted their long chirps and an eerie silence overtook the dusty Louisiana road.

After a moment of the unnatural quiet, a man of around forty, in well-worn clothes and holding a ragged coat in his arm, stood up from beside the road.

He was common in appearance, yet stood tall and held an air of dignity about himself, even in his weathered apparel.

He moved slowly to the road's edge and stood watching down the long stretch of gravel.

Soon, a dark colored Ford sedan came traveling towards him at a rapid pace. The car came into view with a contrail of dust billowing behind.

As soon as the sedan passed by the man, brakes were applied, causing the car to slide a bit and come to a noisy halt about twenty yards past him.

The man beside the road turned, and as if anticipating the arrival of a car, began walking through the dust towards it.

As he came closer, a sweaty young man got out of the front passenger door and walked to the back of the car. He opened the rear driver's side door and looked back down the road to where the man now stood.

"I'm riding back here." The young man said in a rough voice and then climbed into the back seat.

The man walked around to the passenger side of the car and seeing a woman laying in the back seat, he opened the front passenger door.

The driver also appeared rough and had sweat beads on his forehead.

A musk smell, mixed with cigarettes and whiskey resonated inside the interior of the automobile.

Once the doors shut, the young man in the back said, "Let's go Henry," and the driver took off quickly, causing the tires to spin rocks and dust into the air behind them.

Warm air entered the car through the open windows and allowed a small amount of reprieve from the humid Louisiana heat.

Henry was a young man in his early twenties. He appeared nervous as he drove the Ford sedan, glancing towards the man with suspicion in his eyes.

The passenger now noticed that Henry had a pistol sitting between his legs. The edgy young driver looked over towards him again and then glanced at the rearview mirror on the passenger door.

He began to speak in a low, aggressive voice. "Don't be getting any ideas." He again glanced at both side mirrors, as if someone might come up quickly behind them. Then he checked the rearview mirror and continued in the same tone.

"You know that's Bonnie and Clyde back there don't you?"

The passenger glanced back at the two people in the back. They appeared tired and uncomfortable. They seemed to be sleeping or trying to sleep. The passenger turned back to the driver.

"I was just catching a ride. Maybe I should be getting out now." He said politely with a southern drawl.

Henry smirked at this. He again checked the mirrors as the car juggled around from the rough gravel roads. "There ain't anyone getting out now, unless Clyde says so. Or we all die in a hail of bullets."

The passenger again glanced at the pistol between the driver's legs before he turned to the front windshield.

Suddenly a large bug connected violently against the windshield directly in front of him, causing him to flinch. Henry chuckled a little at this. The passenger turned to Henry and watched him a few seconds. He then turned his attention to the scenery passing by outside his window.

After almost an hour of driving, they pulled down a side road. There stood the remnants of a house. From what could be seen, a fire likely destroyed the home and after years of abandonment only fragments of the original structure could be seen.

Henry and the passenger climbed out and began to stretch a little. Clyde exited the rear door of the car and quickly limped around to the other door. He opened this one and carefully assisted Bonnie out. She appeared to have a wounded leg. She limped with Clyde's help to a stump and laid against it.

Clyde pulled two cigarettes from a pack in his pocket. He quickly lit both and handed Bonnie one. She immediately began to pull drags from the cigarette, as if desperate for the nicotine, and then blew the smoke out quickly so she could pull another drag from it. The grayish blue smoke briefly floated around her before disappearing.

After watching this, the older man that was picked up from the roadside found some brick remains of a porch support and sat down facing the two, while Henry scanned the area in a manner to detect any unseen threats.

Clyde retrieved a few things from the back seat of the car and then the trunk. He tucked a pistol under his belt, and placed several bottles of whiskey on a flat area close to Bonnie.

"Go see if you can get some gas, and cigarettes; maybe something to eat too." Clyde sounded winded as he told Henry this.

Henry nodded and left quickly in the car.

Clyde placed a folded jacket behind Bonnie and gave her a drink from a whiskey bottle. She coughed a little after taking a drink. When she coughed she grimaced in pain and held her leg. She lay back on the stump and closed her eyes.

The afternoon waned. Clyde began to move about, gathering pieces of wood and placing them into a pile. The man watched Clyde with apprehension but said nothing. The outlaw in turn continued to glance over at the man from time to time.

The man was older than Clyde. He could see Clyde must be in his early to mid twenties. Yet the young man appeared tired and spent. After several tense moments of watching each other the older man spoke.

"I don't believe I belong here. I'll be moving along."

Clyde sneered at the man. "You may not belong here, but you're here now. You got a problem with the company you keep?"

The older man said nothing but picked up a stick and raked it on the ground in a drawing fashion.

Clyde continued. "You don't look so important to me. What good are you? All the good folks out there that don't want anything to do with Bonnie and me; they all got some occupation they pride themselves highly of. So what is it you're good for?"

The man casually dropped the stick and gazed at the ground when Clyde asked him this. He then folded his ragged coat and repositioned it over his leg in a manner suggesting he wouldn't be leaving soon. After a few seconds he replied to Clyde, but without much zeal.

"I've done some writing over the years. But folks haven't been reading my work much lately. Now days I just seem to wander around here and there; sort of like the wind I suppose, speaking, where folks will have me; in churches and community buildings sometimes. But most folks seem to want someone to talk to rather than do any listening."

Clyde chuckled at this as he knelt down to light some scraps of paper under the small pile of wood.

"Yeah, times are tough all over ain't they? You sound like a preacher to me. That's what all those high and mighty preachers like to do, write stuff and then talk to people. Tell folks how bad they are and how they're all going to hell. Are you a preacher?"

The fire began to slowly blaze as Clyde asked the man this.

"No." The man said, almost in a whisper.

"Yeah, well, I think you're the same thing as a preacher whether you admit it or not."

Clyde blew lightly on the small fire after saying this. The fire became a little larger as he did.

Once the fire took hold and began to burn on its own Clyde stood back up. He walked over to Bonnie and checked on her. She lay asleep, though rustling about occasionally as if uncomfortable.

He then sat back down; staring at the small fire and glancing up at the man from time to time. The evening stressed towards night as the two men eyed each other.

Clyde flipped his cigarette into the fire and stood up. He moved over to the whiskey bottles and picked one up. He took a drink and wiped his mouth on his shirt sleeve. He pulled another cigarette out of the pack with his mouth as he stared across the fire at the man.

Once his cigarette had been lit and he'd taken a long drag from it, he spoke again as he exhaled the smoke and paced slowly around the fire.

"I've been wanting to tell someone the real truth of things. You look like someone that'll know the truth when you see it."

The young outlaw took another long drag and expelled it towards the sky. He thought for a second and then continued.

"You see Preacher, Bonnie and me; we're doing all the good people a favor, even though they don't seem to realize it. We're actually fighting all the corrupt government people and the bankers that take people's land. We should be heroes. The truth of the matter is, the government trains people to go out and kill. And they say it's all right when soldiers do that for the government. But they call Bonnie and me 'murderers.'"

Clyde took another drag from the cigarette as Preacher watched from the other side of the fire. He spewed the smoke out quickly and continued. "And the government takes people's land. They steal good folk's land from them. They kick them off their own land and call that repossession for past due taxes. But they call Bonnie and me 'robbers.' So you see Preacher, we're the good ones, cause we're fighting for all those folks out there that won't fight. That is the truth Preacher, that is the real truth."

Clyde took another drink of whiskey as if to stress his statement before he looked over at Preacher with interest.

Preacher sat silent. He gazed down at his feet and rubbed the worn toe of his shoe in the dirt. Clyde took another long drag from his cigarette and blew the smoke out as he gazed off into the evening sky.

Finally, Preacher looked up at Clyde and in a stern voice asked.

"Is that the truth Clyde? Is that the real truth?"

Clyde froze in place when Preacher asked him this. He turned and stared at Preacher with a slight anger in his eyes. He took another drag from his cigarette and appeared to consider Preacher's question briefly before replying.

"Everybody thinks they know all about the truth. Everyone has their opinion about the truth. But all those opinions are different. The truth is, Bonnie and me are just defending ourselves. I want everyone to know that. That's my truth Preacher. We're just defending ourselves from the law. We're just trying to survive. We're not bad. The law is the one that's bad. If the law would leave us alone there wouldn't be any reason to fight."

He then stared at Preacher in anticipation of an answer. He quickly lifted the bottle up for another drink. He wiped his mouth on his sleeve again then the sweat from his forehead.

Preacher used his forearms to lean on his legs. He gazed down at the ground between them as if searching for some hidden object. Darkness now took over and the fire began to create splashes of light around them.

As seconds passed by and the embers from the small fire danced high into the air, Clyde again glanced at Preacher. He smiled due to the long pause.

But then Preacher took a deep breath and replied with clear and unfaltering words. "You may speak what you consider to be the truth for you and Bonnie. But generally speaking, you're still wrong. And the general nature of that wrong defeats any truth you may hold on your own."

Now Clyde became animated and reacted to Preacher in anger.

"What is that? You tell me Preacher, why you think, what you just said, has anything to do with anything. No one can say what the truth is or isn't. If you know what the truth is then you tell me Preacher. You tell me right now what the truth of anything is."

Preacher never looked up as Clyde said this. Instead he continued to scan the ground between his legs. But after Clyde finished making his statement Preacher casually looked up at him and replied calmly.

"I believe the truth is, every man knows right from wrong deep down inside. And this is a universal truth. Not the truth a person builds up around them by their own deeds. And every man and woman must face this truth in some form or fashion before they die."

Clyde stared at Preacher. He seemed surprised that he actually had an answer. Preacher in turn continued with his assessment after a brief pause.

"Whether people accept this, shall we say, 'spirit of truth' or not, doesn't change it Clyde. Whether a man allows himself to see truth or not won't eliminate its existence. But everyone will face the truth in some way. Each man and woman will have the opportunity to do the right thing. And this fact is one of those 'real truths' that no man will ever be able to alter by his own devices or actions."

Clyde continued to stare at Preacher with contempt. Then he turned to Bonnie. She was sitting up, staring into the fire. Clyde looked back at Preacher and sort of nodded at Bonnie, as if he'd woken her.

"How long have you been up Sugar?"

Bonnie moved a little and grimaced in pain as she did so. "Long enough," she replied flatly. "Give me a cigarette would you?"

Clyde pulled a pack of cigarettes out and lit one. He handed it to Bonnie. Then he sat down beside her and pulled a cigarette out for himself.

Bonnie stared across the fire at Preacher. She pulled a drag from her cigarette and exhaled the smoke quickly.

Clyde handed her the whiskey bottle. She took a drink and her face twisted as she swallowed. Just as she put the cigarette into her mouth again a car could be heard turning down the lonely road.

Clyde stood and pulled the pistol from his belt. He stared with apprehension at the head lights rolling slowly towards them.

"It is Henry." He tucked the pistol back into his belt. Bonnie laid back as she could also see the familiar sedan moving closer.

Henry hopped out of the car, turning the headlights out as he did so.

"Anyone recognize you?" Clyde asked as Henry opened the back door of the car.

"I don't think so. I went to a small store on the edge of town that had just one old man working. He seemed too tired to care about anything."

Preacher noticed that Henry seemed to fear Clyde as much as respecting him. He was also obviously a little younger than Clyde. Preacher sat quietly and watched the unusual relationship with interest. Clyde treated Henry as an employee, but then also seemed to treat him as a grunt at times.

Henry pulled a sack from the back seat. He then pulled various food items and cigarettes out of the bag, setting them down with the items Clyde had beside the fire. As he stood back up Henry glanced over at Preacher. He said nothing to him and Preacher watched Henry with apprehension.

As Clyde and Bonnie began to eat, Henry went back to the car and retrieved another sack. This sack had several large bottles of whiskey and another bottle that Preacher couldn't tell for sure what the contents were.

They sat around the fire eating while Preacher watched. Then Clyde threw part of a loaf of bread over to Preacher.

After examining the loaf on the ground a few seconds, he reached down and gingerly picked it up. He then closed his eyes briefly. After a couple seconds he opened them up and began to eat the bread in small bites. As he did this he glanced over to Clyde who now chuckled under his breath and sneered slightly at Preacher.

Later Clyde, Bonnie and Henry sat around the fire. They smoked cigarettes one after the other. They drank and played cards without stopping. Around midnight Preacher pulled his coat over himself and lay on the ground watching them until finally falling asleep.

The next morning, crackling embers of the dying fire greeted Preacher as he opened his eyes. Dampness persisted in the air. He sat up. The sun had not broken across the horizon yet. There sat Clyde across the smoldering fire, staring at Preacher with hollow, emotionless eyes.

Preacher looked at Bonnie and Henry as they lay asleep with thin blankets tossed over them. As he sat up, Preacher quickly turned his eyes back to Clyde and now refused to turn away or show weakness. Clyde in turn continued to sit stoically; examining Preacher in silence. The two remained in this state for several moments as the others slept.

When the light of the sun broke, causing a few rays to stream across Preachers face, Clyde began to speak in a low voice. He struggled to sound friendly and more civilized than the previous night.

"All the good folks are saying Bonnie and I are killers and bad people. They should know we're just trying to defend ourselves from corrupt law people. Bonnie and I are fighting for all those good folk out there because they don't have the gumption to fight for themselves."

Clyde took a quick drag from his cigarette and continued as the smoke came from his mouth. "Someone like you could tell them our side of it and they would listen to you. If you told the people we're out here fighting their fight, they might listen."

Preacher watched Clyde closely as he said this. Then he replied to Clyde after very little thought.

"I can't tell the people such a thing."

Clyde appeared puzzled by this answer. His voice became more hostile.

"You're supposed to be so good. You said yourself that you do speaking and writing. You said yourself you've attended churches. What do you mean you won't tell the people?"

Preacher picked up a small stone and tossed it into the remnants of the fire, causing tiny glowing embers to fly upwards. Then he replied as he watched the smoldering campfire.

"A man has a right to defend himself from an aggressor just as a country or even a town has the right to defend itself. It does this by asking a few of the citizens to fight the threat for the good of all the people. Are you defending yourself Clyde, or are you the aggressor?"

Preacher paused for a second as if in thought, and then continued.

"Unless the people asked you to fight for them, you ain't fighting for the people. You're fighting for yourself. Did any of those good folk you speak of ask you to do what you're doing?"

Clyde's mouth twisted with anger when Preacher said this. He took another drag from his cigarette and spewed the smoke out.

Just as Clyde was about to also spew a mouth full of curses out, Preacher turned to look at Bonnie. Clyde then also turned and looked at Bonnie. He realized she lay awake, gazing out across the dying fire.

"Give me a cigarette Clyde." She said with a weary voice.

Clyde pulled a cigarette from the pack and lit it for Bonnie. He handed the cigarette to her and she quickly began to pull a drag from it with urgency. He returned to his makeshift sitting spot and stared at Preacher with anger.

Preacher in turn watched Clyde with a quiet resolve. Occasionally he raked a small stick on the ground between his legs but otherwise didn't express weakness to the outlaw.

Soon Henry stirred and after a few bites of leftover food they all began to load into the car. Clyde assisted Bonnie into the back seat and with a flash of Clyde's pistol Preacher once again moved reluctantly to the front passenger seat.

As the car rumbled down the rough back roads Henry turned towards the passenger seat from time to time. Preacher glanced back at Henry but neither said anything. Bonnie smoked one cigarette after another.

64

Clyde continued to nurse a bottle of whiskey. He still seemed angry and when Preacher turned to look at him he still had wrath in his eyes. Eventually Preacher simply watched the scenery go by.

Later in the afternoon they came close to a town. Clyde had Henry pull into a gas station and an attendant filled the car with gas.

Henry went inside and bought several more packs of cigarettes along with some sandwiches.

Preacher noticed Bonnie and Clyde sat in the back attempting to appear normal. They acted as if they were talking together in an effort to avoid revealing their faces to the attendant.

As the attendant washed the windshield he briefly stared straight at Preacher. And then he glanced back at Bonnie and Clyde as the two continued their charade of chatting together.

After the attendant finished with the windshield he moved around to the back of the car and this caused Bonnie and Clyde to relax some.

Preacher again glanced back at Clyde who checked out the back as the attendant continued his work. Clyde turned and looked at Preacher; then pulled his coat away from his waist to reveal his pistol. Preacher turned back to the front of the car and stared out.

After returning to the car, Henry started the sedan up and they drove quietly through the back streets of town. Once on the other side, the car picked up speed and soon they were far away. The Louisiana backwoods swallowed them up as Henry ventured onto familiar roads.

Then he turned down a narrow, seldom traveled road. The grass grew in the middle of this road and only the two wheel tracks could be seen. Under the car the grass brushed the floorboards.

After traveling the primitive road about a half mile, Henry pulled off to the side of a creek and placed the car in a semi-hidden spot behind some small trees and brush. Then everyone wearily climbed out of the car.

A barren area, of around thirty feet, lay beside the creek. It was where the creek had risen and receded causing only rock and small stones to abide now.

"We'll stay here for a little while just in case anyone in town noticed us. Later we can get back on the road. We should still make it back to your Pa's place before dark."

After saying this Clyde helped Bonnie sit beside the car and immediately she lit up a cigarette. Henry nodded in agreement and brought the sandwiches out. Then he pulled several large pieces of logs closer to sit on.

Preacher sat and watched them eat. Again, Clyde watched him closely as if waiting for him to ask for some food. Preacher said nothing, however. When they'd almost finished eating, Clyde reached into the paper bag and pulled out half a sandwich. He sat it on the log and then glanced over to Preacher. He lit up a cigarette as Henry and Bonnie finished their meal. He smoked his cigarette slowly and continued to watch Preacher.

When Henry finished his meal he stood and stretched. "I'm going to go keep watch." He then walked off towards the obscure road.

Clyde nodded. Seeing Bonnie had finished her sandwich he lit another cigarette and handed it to her. She climbed into the back seat of the car and sort of laid back in the seat as she smoked her cigarette.

When everything became quiet, Clyde took the half sandwich and walked over to Preacher. He sat the food down beside him. Then, he walked back over to where he was before and sat back down.

Preacher glanced down at the sandwich. He then looked back at Clyde who again watched him closely as he lit another cigarette from the one he'd just finished.

Several minutes passed by as the two observed each other. Then Preacher reached down to pick up the sandwich. When he did this Clyde straightened a little and took hold of the pistol handle in his belt. Preacher stopped before his hand touched the food beside him.

Clyde sneered a bit and then rubbed the handle of the pistol softly. Preacher slowly moved his hand to the sandwich without showing any emotion, but also never taking his eyes from Clyde.

Picking the food up, Preacher lowered his head a few seconds and then opened his eyes and placed his gaze immediately on Clyde again. He slowly took a bite of the sandwich and chewed with caution. Clyde chuckled and then moved his hand back from the pistol.

As Preacher slowly ate, Clyde reached over and picked up a near-empty bottle of whiskey. He turned the bottle up and finished about half of the remaining liquid in one large drink. Then he wiped his mouth on his sleeve, while grimacing from the taste of the alcohol. Once he'd recovered from the drink he again stared at Preacher.

"That's just like that couple we picked up a while back; all good, upstanding and law abiding citizens. They didn't hesitate to eat food that was bought with stolen money though. All the good people suddenly turn bad when they get hungry."

Clyde paused briefly and then continued.

"You tell me Preacher, why isn't that the truth? You're eating food bought with stolen money. You talk to me about truth and then you eat a sandwich bought with money that was stolen from a bank. Go right ahead Preacher; tell me the truth about that."

After Clyde said this he took another long drag from his cigarette. Again he spewed the smoke out in a rapid exhale through gritted teeth and tight lips. He stared at Preacher and then stood up. He began to pace a little in front of the log.

Preacher finished chewing a bite and gazed at the sandwich, seeming to pay little attention to Clyde.

This pause caused Clyde to become more animated. Now he laughed under his breath as he stared down at Preacher. He turned the bottle up and took another drink leaving only a small amount in the bottle.

Preacher swallowed and without looking at Clyde, began to speak.

"When a soldier is taken prisoner, he doesn't turn down the food offered to him by his enemy simply because the food was grown on enemy soil. The bread did no evil. Nor does food commit crimes. I can give a piece of this bread to a bird and it won't poison the bird. And the bird won't question the origin of the offering either.

"The wrong occurred when you forcefully took the bounty of another man's labor. The fact that your prisoners eat food derived from evil gains won't undo the initial wrong committed. And it doesn't make them guilty of your crime."

Now Clyde's face contorted in a fit of anger. Preacher watched the flush of blood flow to his face, causing his features to express an immediate and evil desire to quench the rage welling up inside him.

Clyde immediately threw the whiskey bottle at Preacher just as a loud cry of violent intent burst from his lungs, "Aaarrhhhhgggggg!" Clyde's aim with the bottle was spot on. Preacher raised his arm just in time to deflect the projectile hurling towards him. The impact of the bottle caused a distinct clunking sound as it made contact, and then fell beside the log.

Preacher grabbed his arm in pain, but he never uttered a sound. He grimaced and held his wound as he kept his eyes on Clyde.

Now the pistol came quickly from behind the belt. Clyde aimed it straight towards Preacher's head.

"You're just asking for a bullet between the eyes Mister. I've shot men for no reason at all. Now you have the nerve to say such things to me? You just want a bullet to the brain don't you?"

Preacher continued to stare at Clyde, as he rubbed his arm from the pain. Then he spoke, but had no fear in his voice.

"You can try to destroy the truth Clyde. You can shoot me and anyone else that speaks the truth, but that won't destroy it. The truth is all around us and inside us. You spoke the truth just now. You've shot men for no reason. That same truth is what convicts you of the murders; because no man in his right mind asks for a bullet between the eyes. You've lived by the gun and I suspect you'll die by it."

68

Clyde cocked the pistol slowly. His hand trembled slightly as he aimed squarely for Preacher's head. At almost the same instant that he pulled the trigger, Clyde moved his aim to the bottle beside Preacher. As the loud gunshot rang out, glass sprayed onto Preacher and around him.

From the back of the car Bonnie jerked up as the gunshot startled her from sleep. She looked out to Clyde and then shouted in a hostile voice.

"Clyde, would you stop doing that? I told you it makes my whole body hurt." She then lay back down with a sound of exasperation.

Henry came running up with his pistol pulled. He looked at the shattered bottle and then Clyde who still held the pistol in the air. Sweat rolled down the side of his head. He slowly put the pistol back into his belt. He sneered at Preacher and turned away from him.

"We should probably be going." Henry said meekly.

Clyde cursed under his breath and went to the back of the car. He opened up the door and nudged Bonnie to get her to move over.

With Henry behind him Preacher went to the passenger side and climbed in, still holding his arm.

Henry gathered everything and stuffed it into the trunk. He quickly checked on Bonnie and Clyde in the back seat, then scanned the area for anything incidentally left behind. The young outlaw moved to the driver's side and climbed in; he started the car and they moved back onto the road.

An hour passed with no one in the car uttering a word.

Then a car came towards them. Dust floated around the back of it as it hurled into view. Police lights on top could be seen and as they passed each other while a sheriff insignia revealed itself on the side.

Clyde checked out the back window until the threat had gone far behind them. "How much longer till we reach your Pa's?"

Henry glanced in the rear view mirror, and then answered Clyde. "A couple hours maybe, it's taking longer on these back roads."

"Find another place to stop. We'll stay off the roads a while and get back on the way before dark."

Henry nodded and began watching for a suitable spot to get off the road.

Soon he pulled the sedan onto an old road. An abandoned house came into view as the afternoon sun lay around the ramshackle home.

Henry stopped the car behind some trees. The doors opened and everyone began to exit the car.

Clyde helped Bonnie over to an area of the porch that hadn't yet broken down. He gently helped her sit and quickly lit a cigarette for her.

Henry and Preacher watched by the car and from a distance. Then Henry leaned back on the hood of the car.

"We'll be at my Pa's house in a few hours." Henry said this as he continued to watch Bonnie and Clyde. "Maybe he can figure something out. You're pushing your luck, you know that don't you?" Henry turned his head slightly towards Preacher; who glanced at Henry and then turned back to Bonnie and Clyde.

"Yeah, maybe your Pa can think of something. But I'm not figuring I'll make it out of this alive anymore." Preacher said as he briefly looked back at Henry. After this he sat down on the running board of the Ford.

Henry lit a cigarette and spewed a cloud of smoke from his mouth.

Clyde walked over to the car. "I'm going for a walk. Keep an eye on Bonnie." He spoke to Henry and never glanced at Preacher. He then walked with a slight limp to the road and soon disappeared from sight.

Henry looked at Preacher as if he should move, so Preacher stood up and began walking over to where Bonnie sat. Henry moved behind him.

Bonnie sat leaning against one of the corner beams. Preacher sat across from her on the ground. Henry remained standing. He smoked his cigarette and looked around nervously. Bonnie flicked her cigarette butt past Preacher.

"Give me another cigarette Henry."

He pulled one from his pack and after lighting it, handed it to Bonnie. She quickly took a long drag from it causing the tip to burn brighter. As Bonnie smoked her cigarette she stared blankly at Preacher.

Henry paced around the area and began to examine the broken down house as a slight breeze moved through. He walked to the side and looked into a broken window. Then he moved to the back.

"Come here." Bonnie said flatly to Preacher.

Preacher looked at her with some apprehension. He slowly stood up and with his tattered coat in hand, moved closer to her.

"Sit down. I'm sure not going to stand to talk to you."

He did as Bonnie said and sat on the ground in front of her.

She took another long drag from the cigarette. Blowing the smoke out in an apparent feminine fashion she stared at Preacher. Then she sort of sat up a little more and leaned over on her knees towards him.

"You know, I've never seen a man stand up to Clyde before." She said this with a sultry voice.

Preacher looked at Bonnie with compassion in his eyes but gave no reply. After a few seconds Bonnie continued.

"If a man were to come along that could stand up to Clyde, I just might be inclined to get away from this." She pulled another drag from the cigarette and blew the smoke into Preacher's face in a flirty manner. Then she smiled and turned her head a little. She gazed out at Preacher from the corner of her eyes.

He lowered his head when she blew the smoke in his face. He then looked at Bonnie again as she gazed at him seductively.

"Yeah, I might go with such a man and start fresh. I might even go to work again. You know I got a lot of tips when I worked as a waitress. I don't know that I would do that again; I hated it. But I might, if such a man were to come along." She then watched Preacher for his response.

A few long seconds passed by as Preacher seemed to consider what Bonnie had revealed to him. Then in a soft but firm tone he replied.

"You and Clyde are wanted dead or alive; but mostly dead Bonnie. They say you'll both be shot on sight the first chance the law gets. You're in fairly bad shape already. Your leg needs medical attention. You can't walk very far without someone's help. Do you really believe you can ever 'start fresh' again?"

Bonnie stared at Preacher with disdain. She appeared as if she were about to cry. Then slowly her face became stretched and lifeless. With a cold voice she began to speak begrudgingly, as if the words were struggling to get out.

"Get away from me. Get away from me right now. I don't want to ever speak to you again."

Preacher seemed saddened by this.

"Bonnie, it's the truth. I'm sorry, but it's the truth."

"Did you here me? I said to get away from me. I don't want to hear anything you have to say." Now her voice became louder. "Get away from me!"

Preacher stood and walked back over to where he sat before just as Henry came around the corner of the house.

Henry looked at Bonnie curiously.

"Give me another cigarette Henry." She said.

He pulled a cigarette from his pack and quickly put it in her outstretched hand.

She instantly lit the cigarette from her previous one with a shaking hand and took a long and desperate drag from it. Then she looked back at Henry as the smoke expelled from her mouth and nostrils.

Henry seemed to wonder if she was all right but neither said anything.

Preacher sat with his legs crossed and laid his coat across his legs.

Soon Clyde came back and sat beside Bonnie. They all sat quietly as the cicadas screeched a constant tune in the trees around them. Henry found some cans of food in the car and they ate from the cans.

As the afternoon turned to evening, Clyde motioned for them to leave and soon the sedan was back on the road.

The sun dropped below the horizon as they pulled into the drive of Henry's father's house. Clyde walked around the car and just as Preacher began to get out he took hold of the door.

"Nope," he said as he lifted up a pair of handcuffs. He motioned for Preacher to move to the back seat behind the driver side, and then put one side on Preacher's wrist in the handcuffs and the other handcuff around the window frame of the car.

"I'm getting sick and tired of looking at you." He clicked the handcuffs closed on the door.

Preacher watched in silence as Clyde did this. But as Clyde began to walk away, Preacher replied. "You may not want to look at me anymore Clyde. But it won't change the fact that I'm here."

Clyde glanced back at Preacher but then quickly moved around to help Bonnie.

Henry's father appeared somewhat happy to see his son again. They all laughed about something as they went up the steps to the house.

Henry's father waited until the others were in. He then turned and looked out to where Preacher sat. He expressed concern as he stared in Preacher's direction. Then he turned back to the house and walked inside.

Outside, in the darkness, Preacher listened and stared at the dim light streaming from the windows. Laughter would erupt, and from the sounds and what little could be seen he determined they were playing cards and drinking.

He sat alone quietly. Clyde had done a sufficient job in restricting him from any interference. Apparently he reminded them of things they wished to not think of.

He moved a little in an effort to get comfortable. The hours slowly slipped by. He placed his ragged coat behind his head and tried to rest.

Later, more laughter and noises of people walking out of the house aroused Preacher. Clyde and then Bonnie came out the door almost stumbling down the steps. Henry and his father walked out of the door behind them.

"Come on. I want to go for a drive. I'm sick of being in the house." Bonnie sounded about half intoxicated.

"That is a great idea Sugar." Clyde replied, not sounding very sober himself.

They moved towards the car and Preacher sat up. When Clyde reached the car he noticed Preacher and suddenly seemed to lose his humor.

Rather than helping Bonnie in the back he asked her if she would rather sit in the front for a while.

"Yeah, that sounds good. I'm getting tired of riding in the back anyway." After saying this Bonnie crawled into the front seat with Clyde's help.

Henry got into the driver's seat and started the car. Clyde unlocked Preacher and then shut his door, then walked around the back of the car and got in the back seat behind Bonnie and beside Preacher.

He looked over at Preacher with a foreboding in his eyes. Preacher pulled his coat from behind his neck and laid it across his legs.

As the sedan rumbled down the gravel roads Clyde would glance over at Preacher. As he pulled a drag from his cigarette, Clyde's face would light up enough to show an ominous expression. Then Bonnie would laugh about something and Clyde would temporarily turn his attention back to Bonnie.

As the night wore on Preacher pulled his coat up over him and leaned back in the corner between the door and the back seat. He closed his eyes as the others talked and drank.

Cigarette smoke swirled around his nose as all three outlaws smoked one cigarette after the other. He drifted into a light slumber and tried to find solace in the vibration of the car as he also attempted to tune out the loud criminals.

Sometime later, Preacher was aroused from his light sleep by the sudden jolt of the car. As he woke up he realized the vehicle must have hit a bump or pothole in the road.

A strange quiet inside the car indicated the three criminals had finally become exhausted. He laid his head back into the corner and glanced over to Clyde.

Clyde sat leaning in the opposite corner of the car in a similar fashion to Preacher. He stared at Preacher with an evil intent. In his hand he held his pistol pointed at Preacher. The rough road caused the barrel of the pistol to waver slightly, but Clyde sat silent, staunchly aiming it straight at Preacher.

He examined the situation while he lay in the corner. He said nothing but gazed into Clyde's eyes. The young outlaw appeared to be desperate and searching for something unseen.

Preacher knew there was little left to say to Clyde which he'd not already said. He waited and watched.

After what seemed to be a many minutes, Clyde began to speak in a low and scornful voice.

"What am I to do about you? I thought if I brought you along, you might help us, but you're no good to me."

Preacher thought a few seconds before replying. Then he spoke in a calm tone.

"It's not my help you want Clyde. You want to manipulate me. You want me to present something false in order to help you justify your actions. Regardless of what you decide to do about me. I won't be beaten down and turned into a living lie."

Clyde now appeared to consider the words before replying, "If you got no use for me, then I got no concern about you."

"There's still time Clyde."

The outlaw seemed puzzled by Preacher's words.

"Time for what?"

"Time to do the right thing," Preacher replied.

This only seemed to anger Clyde even more. He turned slightly to speak to Henry.

"What time is it, Henry?"

Henry acknowledged Clyde's question by a nod. He pulled a cigarette lighter from his jacket pocket and lit it. Then he held it over his watch as he tried to check the time and steer the car. After a few seconds of glancing at his watch Henry answered Clyde.

"It's twelve minutes till midnight."

Clyde looked back at Preacher. He cocked the hammer of the pistol back.

"There's no more time." Clyde pulled the trigger.

The inside of the car lit up as the loud gunshot rang out. The car slid to a halt as Henry slammed on the breaks. Bonnie awoke in a shock and sat up quickly. After realizing they were not being shot at, she instantly became angry.

"Clyde… how many times do I have to tell you to quit that? It makes my leg hurt!"

The back door opened and Preacher fell limp from the car; rolling into the ditch. The door slammed shut and the car sped away into the darkness.

Dawn broke slowly over the horizon and as the warm sun rose higher into the sky a snake crawled cautiously alongside the road and past the motionless body in the ditch. Cicadas began screeching, individually at first, until slowly a chorus of their strange calls erupted in the trees.

Preacher stirred. Slowly he picked himself up. Sitting in the ditch he looked down and carefully examined himself for damage.

He then examined the ragged coat that he had over him when Clyde pulled the trigger. Lifting it up he identified a bullet entrance on one side and the exit on the other side; indicating a bullet passing through the coat but somehow missing him.

After studying his coat, Preacher moved a little farther from the ditch and closer to the cooler shade of a nearby tree. He sat staring out at the barren road. The cicadas became even louder as the sun crept higher into the sky. Still Preacher sat silently staring at the road.

The sun overhead indicated a time of around 10:00 am and the cicadas now screeched with an unrelenting roar of sound. The road silently mocked Preacher as nothing and no one crossed it all morning.

Then, with a shocking urgency the cicadas fell silent. Nothing could be heard. The slight breeze seemed to have also died.

Preacher gazed around but made no move. The eerie silence held true as seconds ticked by.

Then, he slowly stood up and walked to the side of the dusty road. With the battered coat on his arm he put his hands into his pockets and turned to stare down the rugged gravel lane.

Now the cicadas slowly began to screech again. The breeze once again floated slowly through the air and the leaves in the trees fluttered about in a carefree manner.

After a few moments, the sound of a car could be heard. Then it came into view. Preacher watched as it approached. It swerved a little from one side of the road to the other. He stood fast by the road, not moving.

The automobile passed by him and slowed down. Again it swerved and after traveling about a quarter mile the car suddenly slid to a stop beside the road.

Preacher turned and began walking towards the vehicle.

The door opened and a large man in a white suit slid halfway out of the car. As Preacher got closer he watched him with interest.

The man held his chest while leaning over, obviously laboring for breath. He stared at the ground between his feet as he held the place on his chest where his heart would be.

Preacher approached the man and could see he was sweating profusely.

"Are you all right?"

The man turned to Preacher with a taut red face and fear still stretched across it. He then moved his hand inside his suit pocket and pulled out a handkerchief as if in an effort to hide the fact he was holding his chest. He wiped his face gingerly with the handkerchief.

"Yeah, I'm fine."

The man stood with some effort. He leaned on the car and tried to pull himself together.

"It's fiercely hot. I just needed to catch my breath."

Preacher studied the man who appeared to be in his late fifties.

"You headed this way?" The man asked this with a feeble point from his hand.

"Yes, I'm headed that way."

"Come on then. There's no need for you to be out here in the heat, all alone like an orphan."

After saying this he chuckled a little and got back into the drivers seat.

Preacher walked around and climbed into the passenger seat across from the man.

As the car began to move down the road Preacher sat watching the man in a concerned manner as he wiped his forehead often with the handkerchief.

Initially he paid little attention to Preacher. Then, as time went by he seemed to feel better. After a while he started to talk.

"This heat reminds me of a week I spent in New Orleans." He looked over at Preacher and smiled, then continued.

"We had a meeting back in, oh 1920 I believe it was. My partner wanted to go to the Red Light district. He says to me, 'Leonard, we need to go get us a city woman for the night. The wives will never know a thing.'" Then Leonard laughed and looked at Preacher slyly.

"So we went to the Red Light district and let me tell you, I got hold of a sweet young whore. She said she was twenty-one. But I don't think she could have been over seventeen!" He laughed again.

"She wasn't so sweet when I got done with her though!" He smiled as if reminiscing and then wiped the sweat from his brow as he glanced over at Preacher.

Preacher gave no expression as he simply sat listening to Leonard, who now appeared very excited to speak his mind.

As the car rolled down the dusty roads Leonard became more revealing and he confessed with zeal many things to Preacher.

"And he hung in that tree for three days before any of them blacks were brave enough to cut him down. I know for sure, because I went by and checked. You see that's what the Klan is there for; to make sure they don't get too high and mighty."

Leonard expressed pride in the dark things he disclosed to Preacher.

As he spoke, Preacher listened intently but gave no sign of approval nor disapproval. This in turn appeared to make Leonard feel at ease because Preacher didn't object to his deeds.

An hour passed by and Leonard had spoke almost without ceasing the entire time.

Then, they suddenly came upon a mass of cars pulled over to the side of the road. People walked towards something ahead and a few were walking away from the mysterious attraction.

Leonard slowed down and pulled over to the side.

"What in H E double L?" He said this with astonishment as people moved by his window.

When a man passed by in the opposite direction as if he had already seen what lay ahead, Leonard asked him. "What's going on up there?"

The man stopped and moved closer to Leonard's window.

"They gunned down Bonnie and Clyde up the road a bit. The law caught 'em in an ambush. A sheriff and some deputies must have plugged 'em a thousand times. There's blood everywhere. It is like a slaughter house!"

When the man said this Leonard immediately became excited and a smile erupted across his face.

"You don't say, Bonnie and Clyde? I've got to see this."

The man shook his head a little as if feeling ill. "It's a bloody mess. I ain't ever seen anything like it." He then left in the direction he was going before Leonard stopped him.

Leonard opened the door and got out. He looked over to the passenger seat with an anxious expression.

"Ain't you coming to see?"

Preacher said nothing for a few seconds, and then shook his head with an expression of sadness indicating he didn't intend on going.

"Don't you want to see this?" Leonard asked again with some bewilderment.

"Why would any decent person be eager to see such a thing Leonard?"

The smile faded as Leonard considered this. "Well, this is Bonnie and Clyde though; the outlaws."

Preacher stared at Leonard a few seconds.

"They were still human beings."

Now Leonard's eyes dropped as he seemed to be searching for something else. His face twisted a little as he appeared to see something inside himself that was unattractive.

He looked briefly back to the passenger's seat.

"Well, the truth is, I don't ordinarily like to see this sort of stuff. It's not that I enjoy other people's pain."

Preacher looked him straight into the eyes and the two men remained in this state briefly before Preacher finally spoke.

"Is that the truth, Leonard? Is that the real truth?"

Leonard expressed shame on his face now. He turned away from Preacher and stared at the ground briefly. Yet he gave no answer. He then slowly closed the car door and turned to join the mass of people.

Preacher sat alone, as the multitude moved eagerly to the place of the dead.

The End

We hope you enjoyed Bane of the Innocent and Twelve Minutes till Midnight. You may be interested in Ever the Wayward Sky by Oliver Phipps. For your convenience we've added a preview of Ever the Wayward Sky and listed some of his other books here.

Ever the Wayward Sky

Oliver Phipps

Chapter One:
The War is Over, But There's no End in Sight

A light haze lay over the North Carolina ground. Sergeant James Taft stepped out of an officer's tent.

"Yes Sir, I will, first thing this afternoon." He replied while moving from the entrance.

As soon as he was completely outside, he became aware of something unusual. The low sound of cheering began to erupt on the far side of the camp. Sergeant Taft turned towards the strange sounds just as his lieutenant stepped out from the tent behind him.

Both men were around the same height and build; five foot ten inches, more or less. However, Sergeant Taft had short dark hair that wasn't curly and unruly as the lieutenants' was. And, James also wore a mustache and goatee, which was popular among the Union cavalrymen.

"What's going on, Sergeant?" The lieutenant moved up beside James, and both watched as a spontaneous celebration appeared to be overtaking the entire camp.

"I don't know, Sir. But it seems to be moving this way." As Sergeant Taft said this, soldiers walked at a rapid pace closer to the two men. They yelled and shouted along the way. One man came swiftly towards them, waving his hat and cheering loudly.

"What's going on soldier?" The lieutenant asked when the man came closer.

"Lee surrendered, Sir. He surrendered to General Grant." Then the man jogged away, shouting and jumping as he went.

The lieutenant looked at Sergeant Taft, who looked back at him. They both seemed to be in disbelief. Then, as more and more soldiers came running through the camp shouting, both men began to smile. They turned and shook hands; congratulating each other for surviving.

James Taft had seldom thought or believed the war would end. After more than four years of fighting, he had a difficult time accepting this reality. As the next few weeks went by, however, the twenty-three-year-old sergeant began to accept that he had indeed survived the war.

Eventually, his unit, the 9th Pennsylvania cavalry began to muster out in Kentucky.

"What are you going to do now, Sergeant?" A young private asked James as they left the headquarters building. Sergeant Taft examined his discharge papers. He seemed to be a bit confused and disoriented.

"I'm not sure, Private."

"You're not sure? Ain't you going home, Sergeant?"

"I suppose I will. What are you going to do?"

The private laughed. "Oh, I got so many things I'm going to do! The first thing is, I'm going to marry my sweetheart, Dolly. Oh, she is a beauty! You got a sweetheart, Sergeant?"

James glanced at the young man.

"No, I don't suppose that I do, Private."

The young man laughed again. "You should get you a sweetheart."

The man stayed with James as they turned in gear and finished other various tasks to complete their discharge. He spoke with almost no restraint. James didn't care though as his mind was absent of anything to talk about.

He felt lost as he said goodbye to his horse. He felt naked as he turned in his revolver and rifle. The saber he'd bought with his money, he gladly packed it with his other meager belongings.

James couldn't seem to break away from the numbness that had taken over him. During his trip home to Pennsylvania, he again became lost in thought. He remembered those he knew that had died in battle. He considered the men he had killed in combat. They wouldn't be going home, ever. They still lay on the battlefield in the cold earth. The war was over. Why couldn't he be glad like so many others? Why did he feel that he shouldn't be leaving the army and yet at the same time, feel that he could not endure any more of the savage brutality he had gone through for four and a half years?

His hometown presented a celebratory atmosphere as James stepped off the train. Banners were hung all around, welcoming the victorious soldier's home.

"James, James Taft! Welcome, home James! My, my, I barely recognized you. You were, what, eighteen when you enlisted? You've grown into quite the man, and hero for that matter."

"Thank you, Mr. Carleton." James shook the man's outstretched hand as a small band struck up the Battle Cry of Freedom. A few of the town women handed out baked items, and one of them poured a cup of black coffee for him.

He looked over the small train station as he sipped the coffee. It hadn't changed much over the years. Yet everything seemed different now.

An elderly lady approached him.

"Your mama is going to be so happy to see you, James! She came down here several times hoping you would arrive with some of the other boys that were coming home. But you've all been coming home a few at a time now after the main group returned."

James smiled at the woman; she had aged considerably in appearance since he last saw her.

"Yes Mrs. Johnson, the cavalry had some extended duties to perform. It took a bit longer for us to muster out."

"Well, no matter. I know she'll be very happy to see you. We're all so proud of you boys."

Mrs. Johnson then took her small handkerchief and put it close to her eye. "It's just a shame we lost so many good young men to that," she acted as if she wanted to say something else, but then continued, "that, terrible war."

James tried to sound compassionate. "Yes Mrs. Johnson, I agree."

"Well James, you tell your mother and the rest of your family hello for me. And we're just so glad to have you back."

Mrs. Johnson then went to speak with another soldier that had also returned on the train.

James moved out of the station and began walking through the Pennsylvania town that he'd grown up in. Memories rushed back to him as he passed buildings and landmarks. Some of the memories brought emotional feelings of his father, who had died when James was only fourteen.

"James? It surely is, young James Taft!" An elderly man in an old suit came up quickly to him with an excited expression on his face.

"Hello, Dr. Weston," James said with not nearly as much excitement as he shook the extended doctors' hand.

"James, it is so good to have you back. I'm sorry you didn't get the big parade and all. We had a big to do when our boys from the regiment returned. I wish you could have come home to that."

"It's alright Doc. Mr. Carleton and some of the ladies met us at the station."

"Well, that's good, James. We've tried to have someone at the station as you boys continue to come in."

"I believe we'll be some of the last, Doc," James replied.

The doctor looked down and shook his head a little. "It seems we've lost so many." Then he glanced back up to James. "Do you need a ride out to your place? I can have the horses hooked up to my carriage."

James smiled. "Thank you, Doc, but I would like to walk. I could use a good long stroll."

"Alright James, I understand."

As he moved on out of town and towards his boyhood home, a dark feeling came over him. He gazed over at the "swimming hole" that he and his brother John had swum many times in. Now the laughter he remembered seemed so far away. His heart felt as if it could no longer recover such a joyful time. The death he had seen and dealt with now anchored him to a place neither high nor low. He simply existed.

He continued towards the family home and memories fluttered through his mind. Races with his brother and friends; some of whom now lay buried in the earth of a distant battlefield. Still, James couldn't shake off the darkness to receive the warm thoughts he desired. Maybe, the sight of his home and his mother would stir the embers of joy that he hoped were still in his heart, somewhere.

Slowly the two-story house came into view. As James moved closer, he became frightened. He slowed down and felt a sense of dread. How could a man who had been in more battles than he could recall be terrified of returning home?

James stopped. He stood at a distance from the house. As his heart beat faster, his mind struggled for an answer. Slowly, the problem began to unravel as he searched his very soul. The questions revealed their ugly presence in his thoughts.

Would they see the terrible things? Would his mother sense the blood and death on him? Would his nephew and niece feel the heat of the hell he had passed through, time and time again? Surely, they would know. He started walking again but felt the weight of these concerns with every step he took. Sweat dripped along the side of his head as these thoughts entrenched themselves into his fears.

With the reluctance, he had felt before racing into a battle, James forced himself to continue moving forward. The aging house came into view as did his niece who was outside. She had grown much since the last time he had seen her. The years had changed her dramatically from the four-year-old girl he remembered. She had her back to him and was kneeled over, picking wildflowers.

James stood outside the small wooden fence that was in obvious need of repairs. He watched his niece in silence as she hummed and picked the flowers one by one. He felt himself trembling in anticipation of her noticing him. Would she scream in fear? Would she see the things he had been through and cry from sadness?

He wanted to do something to let her know that he was behind her, but he felt too frightened to do anything. Then, as she turned, she noticed him standing outside the fence. She stared at him for several seconds with a slightly startled expression. James smiled a little smile at her.

"Uncle James?" She took several small steps towards him as she asked this.

"Hello, Grace." He said to her, relieved that she couldn't see the wariness inside him.

Grace cautiously walked over to the fence. She then extended her handful of flowers to him. James took the flowers and softly said. "Thank you."

"We've been waiting for you Uncle James." As she said this, James' mother stepped out to the front porch and immediately put her hand to her mouth and began to weep.

"James...!" She moved quickly down the porch towards him. His brother now came out and then his wife, with their son behind her. All of them began to say his name and rush to hug him.

Later, he sat in the main room. Everyone sat around him as if he was about to tell a grand tale. His sister-in-law brought him a drink.

"We've been hoping you would show up any day now James." His brother John said and then continued.

"Ma waited at the train station again and again when the regiment began to arrive, but no one could tell us anything about the 9th. We finally stopped going to the station. No one seemed to know anything about the cavalry."

James took a drink and sat the glass on a table beside him.

"Well, we had some extra duties to take care of. We watched over some of the larger reb units as they surrendered. I didn't know how long it would be or I would have written and let everyone know."

His mother appeared to glow from joy.

"No matter, James. We're just so happy to have you back, son."

"Yeah, James, we'll get this place back into shape in no time with you back!" His brother John added.

James smiled a little. He felt strangely out of place sitting peacefully with his family.

"Yeah, we'll do that John." He picked up his drink, more from being nervous than needing it.

As he took a sip, his mind searched for the reason he felt so uncomfortable. He didn't want to talk about farming. He didn't want to think about getting the place back into shape. He felt depressed even considering these things.

Then, with no warning, his nephew Johnny unexpectedly asked a question.

"Did you kill a bunch of Reb's Uncle James?"

John immediately reprimanded his son as everyone looked around in shock.

"Johnny, don't ask such a thing!"

"Why Pa, I want to know?"

A strange sensation swept over James, and he had to get up. He then replied with obvious discomfort, "That's alright, John... I think I'll get some air for a few minutes."

He left the room as the others tried to explain to young Johnny why he shouldn't ask such questions. James stepped out onto the porch and sat down on the steps, in the dark.

His heart beat rapidly. He realized something terrible now. Only when Johnny asked him that question did he feel alive again. What was wrong with him? He ran his fingers through his hair.

John stepped out on the porch behind him. He sat down beside his younger brother.

"I'm sorry James. He's just... so young."

"No, it's alright. I just needed some air. I'm not used to being inside. We slept under the stars as much as we did anywhere else."

John glanced over at his brother. He took a deep breath of the moist night air.

"I wanted to join up, but with Pa gone and two young children."

"No... John. You did the right thing. You're the real soldier for taking care of Ma and this place. I'm sorry that I ran off and left you like I did. I had visions of being some hero, I suppose."

The two men sat quietly for a few minutes and stared out over the dark fields in front of them. Then John said with a softened voice.

"Sounds like your unit had it pretty rough. Up against Forrest and Morgan, seems the 9th took on some of the toughest."

"Yeah, I guess we got our share of it," James replied.

"Well, at least you didn't leave anything out there on the battlefield." John then slapped James on the leg. He stood up and walked back into the house. James then said in a small voice, to himself.

"I'm not so sure of that."

As the days passed, James felt himself sinking further into depression. He tried to work on the family farm but couldn't focus on the tasks. Darkness slowly began to swallow him from the inside out.

"Well, we finally pulled that old stump out of the South field." John attempted to sound encouraging at the dinner table.

"That's wonderful. That old tree always irritated your Pa. I'm glad we took care of it, and it's gone for good." His mother glanced over at James after saying this.

Her son sat staring blankly at his plate of food. He heard nothing they had said.

His mother turned and looked across the table at John, who then glanced over at his wife, Velma. All three now watched James as he held his fork over his food and appeared to be far away.

The two children took notice of what was occurring and began watching their Uncle also.

Realizing the children were watching, Velma stood up and took a pitcher of water over to James.

"Would you like some more water, James?"

He almost shook as he came out of the apparent trance.

"Oh, no Velma, thank you."

Johnny laughed a little, and this caused Grace to giggle as well.

"You children eat now. No playing."

"Yes, Grandma." Both children replied, almost in unison.

James looked around the table with a lost expression on his face.

"I think it'll rain tonight," John said in an attempt to bring supper back on track. "What do you think James?"

"Yes, it might."

He knew something wasn't right. He realized now that he'd been somewhere else. He didn't know what to do about it, though. He glanced around at his family. He loved them dearly, but he didn't belong here. He wasn't sure where he belonged, but he knew now that it wasn't here.

Later, as James lay down to sleep, the rain began. The soft pattering of raindrops outside his window caused a soothing effect, and he drifted into sleep. Then the thunder came, and as James slipped farther into slumber, he found himself on a faraway battlefield again. As the sounds of the storm erupted outside, the cannons roared on the battlefield of James' dream.

"I heard them was Morgan's boys over there, Sergeant."

A young private nervously spoke to Sergeant Taft, who was riding back and forth in front of the men. James reined his horse in to answer the young cavalryman.

"Don't matter who they are, Private! That cavalry unit is protecting the Reb's flank, and we'll run them off the battlefield, or die trying!"

When James said this, the private appeared to calm down. But he was still obviously frightened. All the soldiers appeared concerned. The horses moved underneath them nervously; sensing death to be close at hand. Smoke from the guns drifted through the unit's ranks as James scanned the faces of his men.

He then moved closer to the young private. James thought he might be able to say something to calm the young man, but as he came near, the soldier began to speak.

"I sure got the feeling that I'm going to be one of those that die trying, Sergeant. You ever get that feeling?"

James reined in his mount again, trying to calm it. The horse quivered under him in an apprehensive excitement for the battle at hand. Then, James lied to the young private. He always lied in these situations.

"Almost every day, Private." After James had said this, the man calmed some more. He smiled a little. James smiled slightly as well, and then he thought of several other men that had told him the same sort of thing over the years. They all died on the battlefield after telling him this. The cracking of rifle and cannon fire became intense. He positioned his horse to the front of the unit, ready for battle.

Their lieutenant rode swiftly up from the back of the unit.

"Alright boys, it's time, let's give'em hell."

The lieutenant then pulled his saber out and nodded to their bugler, who immediately sounded the charge. Sergeant Taft spurred his horse just as the lieutenant charged forward.

"Let's go 9th," James yelled out, and his heart began to pound inside his chest.

The ground began to tremble as the horses burst into a gallop.

James looked across the field at the enemy just as bullets began to sing around him.

He became hot as the blood rushed to his head. Then, as always, he slowly became numb as the specter of death approached.

He put the reins in his mouth and lowered his head as if facing a fierce wind. He could now see the enemy's faces clearly.

As the gap closed, he pulled his saber out with his left hand and his revolver out with his right.

The famed "Rebel yell" could be heard from the opposing forces, sending chills down his back.

Now everything began to happen at lightning speed. The two cavalry units collided with the ferocity of a train wreck. As he moved into the Confederates' ranks, he swung his razor-sharp saber and took a Rebels' head almost entirely off from the shoulders. He then turned to his left and fired his pistol into the chest of another, removing the man from his horse in the process.

The sound of bullets flying by him mixed with bodies being struck and cries of pain, all mingled with anger, leather, and metal striking metal.

Another rebel rode up to his right. He was young, and James could see the fear in his eyes. He fired his pistol, but James anticipated it just in time to move. The bullet whizzed by so close that he felt the heat. He maneuvered his saber as the young soldier attempted to cock his pistol again. He lunged the blade forward and felt the steel sink into the mans' body. He watched briefly as the soldier realized James had just ended his life.

He pulled the blade from the man and turned to his left as another soldier was about to fire his rifle at him. James quickly aimed and instinctively fired his cocked pistol. The soldier leaned back as the bullet hit him, firing the gun into the air before falling from his horse.

The enemy was all around him now. He shot another Rebel from his horse. Another one rode toward him as if to avenge his comrade. James shot him also as he tried to swing his saber.

He wanted to get out of the enclosed fighting. He maneuvered his mount to the right, then ran another rebel through the back with his saber. He struggled to pull the blade free as the soldier fell backward onto it.

A bullet cut through the side of his coat making contact with his flesh. He remained on top of his horse. He spotted the enemy that fired the shot. He aimed his revolver and shot as the soldier tried to shoot again. James' shot almost removed the soldier's head.

He pressed his right arm against the wounded side as the pain came. Angered, he spurred his horse forward. He swung his blade and the contact nearly took a passing rebel's arm off.

Another rebel rode toward him at a furious pace, seeming ready to take James down with his saber. James lifted his pistol and shot him from his horse. Then he immediately ran his blade into the side of another rebel that had moved close to him.

James sensed another enemy soldier taking aim; the shot intended for the young private he had spoken with before the start of the battle. James lifted his pistol and pulled the trigger. The clicking of an empty revolver was all he heard. As the young private turned, he would see the bullet from the enemy that would kill him. James yelled out.

"Noooo...!!!"

He cocked the pistol again as the rebel fired. The young private jerked back as the bullet slammed into his chest. James again pulled the trigger; again, and again, the clicking of an empty pistol.

"James?"

The Rebel then turned towards him, and everything slowed down. James raised his saber as the hot blood flowed to his head and caused a flash of anger inside him.

"James, are you alright?"

The battlefield began to fade. James slowly saw his room by the light of a lamp that his mother held. He found himself sitting on the edge of his bed. His left arm raised as if he were holding a saber, while his right arm was elevated halfway and pointed from his body in a manner suggesting a pistol ready to be used.

He blinked several times and looked to his mother, who stood in the doorway with a lamp. She appeared very concerned. Then, John stepped up behind her. As James lowered his arms, Grace and Johnny stepped to the door to see what the commotion was. At last, Velma stepped to the door behind John.

"I guess I was dreaming. I'm sorry if I disturbed anyone."

"Come on children; Uncle James just had a dream." His mother attempted to usher the children away from the doorway. John seemed to want to say something but couldn't find the words. Velma turned and went back towards their bedroom. Finally, John spoke in a nervous tone.

"Well, good night James. I'll uh... I'll see you at breakfast." he then waved slightly and left for his bedroom.

James sat in silence on the edge of the bed. His heart continued to race long after everyone had settled back into their beds. He told himself that he hated the battlefield. The smell of smoke and blood still permeated his nostrils, even though it was only a dream. And yet here he sat, on the edge of the bed, in darkness and silence, reliving the vivid dream over and over in his mind. He wanted to be there again, and this frightened him more than any battle ever did.

As the morning light slowly peeked over the horizon, James' mother stepped out onto the porch where her son sat in a weathered chair. He gazed out to the horizon and only glanced away as his mother sat down across from him.

Several minutes had passed before either spoke. His mother began, softly, but seeming to struggle for her words.

"I wish... well, I just wish your father were here, James. He would be so much better with something like this."

James glanced at her and smiled a little. He then turned back to watch the morning sun creeping up. After a few seconds, he spoke with a slow but resolved tone.

"I never really thought about what I would do after the war, Ma. Because I never believed, I would live through it." He paused and his mother looked down a little as if his words pained her some. He then continued with the same tone.

"I can't stay here. This... staying in one place, it's doing something to me. I'm not for certain what, but it's not good, I know that."

His mother continued to gaze down at the porch, appearing to almost cry. After several seconds, she straightened and again spoke softly.

"You shouldn't run from your problems, Son."

He turned to his mother and examined her face. He loved her so much and wanted to make her understand that he had no desire to leave. He tried desperately to find the words. She looked back to her son with a hope that he might be able to stay. But as she gazed into his eyes, James realized what he needed to say.

"I'm not running from them, Ma. I've got to charge them, at full gallop. It's the only thing I know how to do now. I've got to meet them out there... somewhere, and overcome them, or die trying. I don't know what the outcome will be, but I know now what happens if I stay here."

A tear ran down his mother's face as she realized his words were true, and she would once again be losing her son. She put her head down and wiped the tear away. She nodded a little as another tear dropped to her lap.

Later that morning, John approached his brother, who had walked to the creek. James sat on a large rock, the same one the two had used as young boys to jump into the water.

"It's been a long time since you and I went swimming here." John then sat down beside his brother.

James turned and glanced at him. He then looked back to the creek and tossed a small stone in, as if he'd been waiting for a reason to throw it into the water.

"Yeah, feels like a different lifetime. I've been thinking about those days; before..." James acted reluctant to even say the word.

"Before the war..." John said, with the tone of a big brother. He obviously wanted to confront the problem and resolve it.

James sensed this, but knew the problem was not as simple as removing a tree stump.

"Yeah, before the war," he replied without looking up.

Again, the silence prevailed and the soft flowing creek, along with a few birds was the only sounds heard. Finally, John felt the need to say something.

"Ma says you're going to leave?"

James reached down and picked up another small stone, then replied.

"I can't stay here any longer, John. The war did something to me. I don't know what, exactly, but I know I've got to move. If I don't, I'll get sick."

John looked over at his brother and tried to find an answer. He could think of nothing to change his brother's mind. With no solution in sight, he decided to do what he could to be a friend.

"Where are you planning on going to?"

James glanced at John and felt glad his brother was trying to understand. He tossed the small stone into the creek.

"West, there's a lot of room to move around, out that way. I saved most of my pay from the Army, so I should have enough to get me by for a while. I'll give Ma some money before I leave. I know it won't be the same as having an extra hand around, but maybe it'll help some."

John could only nod in agreement. He knew his brother would stay if he were able to. He patted James' leg and stood up.

"Will you be coming to dinner?"

"Yeah, I'll be back later, before dinner."

John nodded and began walking back towards the house. James again stared at the creek, as if it might answer some of the questions in his mind.

As the sun crept up towards noon, James left the small waterway and went back to the house. He decided he would leave as soon as he could get a good horse and the proper equipment together for an extended trip out West.

Over the next several days he purchased a good mount and all the necessary gear, including two brand new Colt Army revolvers and a Henry rifle.

The departure day came, and he said his good-byes, then moved down the road, away from the house where he had grown to be a young man.

Upon reaching the creek, he turned the horse around and looked back at his home in the distance. He didn't want to leave it. But in his heart, James knew he had to. Something inside him would not rest. The battle within had to run its course, somewhere and somehow. Staying here would only worsen the situation and disrupt the family he loved. With this thought in mind, he turned his horse and moved down the road, towards the struggle he knew he must face. Out there, in the West, somewhere, an unseen enemy awaited him.

We hope you enjoyed Bane of the Innocent and Twelve Minutes till Midnight. You may be interested in other works by Oliver Phipps. For your convenience we've listed some of his other books here.

Ghosts of Company K: Based on a True Story

Tag along with young Bud Fisher during his daily adventures in this ghostly tale based on actual events. It's 1971 and Bud and his family move into an old house in Northern Arkansas. Bud soon discovers they live not far from a very interesting cave as well as a historic Civil War battle site. As odd things start to happen, Bud tries to solve the mysteries. But soon the entire family experiences a haunting situation.

If you enjoy ghost tales based on true events then you'll enjoy Ghosts of Company K. This heartwarming story brings the reader into the life and experiences of a young boy growing up in the early 1970s. Seen through innocent and unsuspecting eyes, Ghosts of Company K reveals a haunting tale from the often unseen perspective of a young boy.

Where the Strangers Live

When a passenger plane disappears over the Indian Ocean in autumn 2013, a massive search gets underway.

A deep trolling, unmanned pod picks up faint readings and soon the deep sea submersible Oceana and her three crew members are four miles below the ocean surface in search of the black box from flight N340.

Nothing could have prepared the submersible crew for what they discover and what happens afterwards. Ancient evils and other world creatures challenge the survival of the Oceana's crew. Secrets of the past are revealed, but death hangs in the balance for Sophie, Troy and Eliot in this deep sea Science Fiction thriller.

A Tempest Soul

Seventeen year old Gina Falcone has been alone for much of her life. Her father passed away when she was young. Her un-affectionate mother eventually leaves her to care for herself when she is thirteen.

Though her epic journey begins in 1920 by an almost deadly mistake, Gina will find many of her hearts desires in the most unlikely of places. The loss of everything is the catalyst that brings her to an unimagined level of accomplishment in her life.

Yet Gina soon realizes it is the same events that brought her success that may also bring everything crashing down around her. The new life she has built soon beckons for something she left behind. Now, the new woman must find a way to dance through a life she could have never dreamed of.

Diver Creed Station

Wars, disease and a massive collapse of civilization have ravaged the human race of a hundred years in the future. Finally in the late twenty- second century, mankind slowly begins to struggle back from the edge of extinction.

When a huge "virtual life" facility is restored from a hibernation type of storage and slowly brought back online, a new hope materializes.

Fragments of humanity begin to move into the remnants of Denver and the Virtua-Gauge facilities, which offer seven days of virtual leisure for seven days work in this new and growing social structure.

Most inhabitants of this new lifestyle begin to hate the real world and work for the seven day period inside the virtual pods. It's the variety of luxury role play inside the virtual zone that supply's the incentive needed to work hard for seven days in the real world.

In this new social structure a man can work for seven days in a food dispersal unit and earn seven days as a twenty first century software billionaire in the virtual zone. As time goes by and more of the virtual pods are brought back online life appears to be getting better.

Rizette and her husband Oray are young technicians that settle into their still new marriage as the virtual facilities expand and thrive.

Oray has recently attained the level of a Class A Diver and enjoys his job. The Divers are skilled technicians that perform critical repairs to the complex system, from inside the virtual zone.

His title of Diver originates from often working in the secure "lower levels" of the system. These lower level areas are the dividing space between the real world and the world of the virtual zone. When the facility was built, the original designers intentionally placed this buffer zone in the system to avoid threats from non-living virtual personnel.

As Oray becomes more experienced in his elite technical position as a Diver, he is approached by his virtual assistant and forced to make a difficult decision. Oray's decision triggers events that soon pull him and his wife Rizette into a deadly quest for survival.

The stage becomes a massive and complex maze of virtual world sequences as escape or entrapment hang on precious threads of information.

System ghosts from the distant past intermingle with mysterious factions that have thrown Oray and Rizette into a cyberspace trap with little hope for survival.

Tears of Abandon

Several college friends start planning a two week kayak trip down an Alaskan river during the summer of 1992. Soon, there are five young people headed to Alaska for a river expedition.

As the trip unfolds and the group gets farther into the wilderness a strange whispering sound attracts their attention. The wonderful vacation begins to take a turn for the worse when they follow the sounds and find something long lost and quiet unexpected.

The Bitter Harvest

The year is 1825, and a small Native American village has lost many of its people and bravest warriors to a pack of Lofa; huge beasts humanoid in shape but covered with coarse hair. The creatures are taller than any normal man, and fiercer than even the wildest animal.

Rather than leave the land of their ancestors, the tribe chooses to stay and fight the beasts. But they're losing the war, and perhaps more critically, they're almost without hope.

The small community grasps for anything to help them survive. There is a warrior on the frontier known as Orenda. He's already legendary across the west for his bravery and honor.

Onsi, a young villager, sets out on a journey to find the warrior.

Orenda will be forced to choose between almost certain death, not just for himself, but also his warrior wife Nazshoni and her brother Kanuna, or a dishonorable refusal that would mean annihilation for the entire village.

The crucial decision is only the beginning, and Orenda will soon face the greatest test of his life; the challenge that could turn out to be too much even for a warrior of legend.

Ever the Wayward Sky

The Civil War is over. But for Sergeant James Taft, there seems to be no end in sight. He had seldom considered what he would do after the war, because he never believed he would live through it.

James briefly returns to Pennsylvania in an unsuccessful attempt to work as a farmer. He then sets out to find peace and somehow vanquish the ghosts in his soul. What he can't possibly see before him as he rides west, is the epic story of tragedy, triumph and finding oneself.

"It's unfortunate, but true, that darkness must often be complete, before we notice the subtle glimmer of hope." - Doc Jefferies, Ever the Wayward Sky.

The House on Cooper Lane: Based on a True Story

It's 1984 and all Bud Fisher wants to do is find a place to live in Madison Louisiana. With his dog Badger, they come across a beautiful old mansion that was converted into apartments.

Something should have felt odd when he found out nobody lived in the apartments. To make matters worse, the owner is reluctant to let him rent one. Eventually, he negotiates an apartment in the old historic house but soon finds out that he's not quite as alone as he thought. What ghostly secret has the owner failed to share?

It's up to Bud to unravel the mysteries of the upstairs apartments, but is he ready to find out the truth?

www.ingramcontent.com/pod-product-compliance
Lightning Source LLC
Chambersburg PA
CBHW020141150626
46552CB00021B/1073